The Wrong Idea

Reading order

The Wrong Idea

THE BANK ROBBERS BOOK 2

ANNIKA MARTIN

Chapter One

"JOHN AND FRANNY TYLER," THOR SAID TO THE HOTEL desk clerk, handing over two driver's licenses.

I smiled brightly, hoping she wouldn't notice anything weird about our very fake documents. We'd gotten them together in a mad rush; we hadn't expected to be on the run today.

On the upside, my awesome curly wig matched the picture perfectly, and Thor was very convincing in his backwards baseball cap, just the thing to match the bro look he had going as John Tyler.

The fakery worked like a charm.

The woman handed over our keycards and pointed us to the elevators.

I let out a breath that I didn't know I was holding and grinned at my fabulous fake husband.

If somebody was able to go back in time and show young me a video of the future where I was checking into a luxurious hotel with Thor, I would never have believed it.

I was a poor sheep farmer with a part-time bank job, struggling to care for my sisters. So, a fancy, glittering hotel—in Los Angeles of all places?

No way.

And a pretending to be married to a man who looked like Thor?

Please.

Handsome didn't even begin to describe Thor. With his blond hair and his athletic physique, my Nordic bandit was molten-lava-level hot.

His hotness had the power to melt faces, to topple walls, to change the topology of vast swaths of land.

Just no way.

You couldn't expand my mind widely enough to contain such a possibility.

And if you'd informed past-me that, yes, it was, in fact, real, and that I'd been whisked out of my monotonous life by three gorgeous, brilliant, kinky bank robbers? And that I'd experience unimaginable thrills with them?

It would've seemed like a dream.

In many ways, it *was* a dream.

Unfortunately, dreams have a way of changing on a dime.

And there was definitely trouble brewing in our little paradise —and not the good kind.

Thor turned to me, pretending to fumble with his bag. "Odin just arrived. He's in the lobby. See him? Left side by the palm."

I glanced over and spotted Odin. "Mmm."

Odin was in disguise, too. He wore a velvet track suit, sunglasses, and a large, unfortunate mole on his left cheekbone. I'd helped him pick out the mole this morning. It had seemed like too much, what with the size of it and the hairs sticking out of it, but Odin was pulling it off.

Odin looked good in anything.

He'd come in a different vehicle, of course. We were being all kinds of careful because my guys' enemy, ZOX, had likely figured out by now that I was more than a passing acquaintance of the trio.

Even worse: they had a photo of me.

We needed to figure out next steps.

It was bad that they had the photo of me—really, really bad.

They could use the photo to figure out my identity, which would give them a new way to get to my guys—and yes, I was thinking of them as my guys at this point.

My biggest fear was that ZOX would track down my sisters at the farm and threaten them as a way to gain leverage over us. Or once my guys sent me home—an idea that I hated—ZOX could always go after me, too…if they were to learn my identity.

ZOX would do just about anything for leverage over Zeus, Odin, and Thor.

So we had to prevent them from learning who I was.

Thor and I paused at the elevator until Odin caught up to us. I hit the button and the three of us got in and rode up in silence, acting like strangers for the elevator cameras.

Finally, we reached our room. Odin collapsed on the bed.

"Did you get them all?" I asked.

Over the last twenty-four hours, Odin had been hacking into lots of social media accounts belonging to me and other people that I knew, grabbing and subtly altering every photo of me possible, changing my face just enough to confuse the photo recognition software that ZOX was surely using.

"Almost done," he said. "Facebook and Instagram have been handled. The DMV, of course. The picture on the farm website. I hit your grade school and high school photos, and luckily nobody took many pictures of you at the bank. What worries me is the photos we don't know about."

"Right." That was the big worry. I set my bags in one of the rooms. We'd gotten a huge suite, as usual, with a sweeping view of red roofs and palm trees and mountains in the distance. "I'll keep thinking and adding to the list."

"Did Zeus make contact yet?" Thor asked.

Zeus had gone back to my little town in order to protect my

sisters from afar, just in case the worst happened—aka if big bad ZOX figured out who I was and went after them.

Things still felt a little weird between Zeus and me, and I couldn't help but wonder if it would always feel that way.

"He called an hour ago," Odin said. "He's been all over that place and lurking around your farm. Nothing's going on. Well, nothing aside from the expected."

The *expected*.

I sighed.

The expected was my sisters being frantic about me having been taken away as a hostage last month during a robbery at the bank where I worked—a *takeover robbery*, as they say in the biz. They'd been worried out of their minds, of course, and in constant contact with law enforcement. They even went on TV to plead for my release.

"How do they seem?" I asked. "Did he say?"

"They're getting back to work," Odin said. "The younger one is back in school, and Zeus has been monitoring that."

"Good," I said. It was good that she was back. "And nobody suspects him?"

"Zeus is an elite operative who has infiltrated heavily guarded enemy compounds. He can blend into a sleepy little town and keep tabs on some farm girls."

I nodded. Of course he could do that. I could only imagine how heavily armed he probably was. He'd get my sisters out of there if ZOX showed up.

But long term? I didn't know what we'd do.

Thor grabbed a ginger-ale from the minibar. He twisted off the cap and tossed it across the room into the garbage, making a clean shot of it.

My bandits were good at everything. It was impressive, but also sad, because they *had* to be good at everything. You can't slip up when you're a fugitive. That's when you die.

"The good news is that I might have a lead on the photo they got," Odin said. "We need to see how bad this is."

"A lead on the photo? From who?" Thor asked.

"From Tabby. We're meeting her tonight," Odin said.

"Does Tabby have a copy of the photo, or just a way to get one?" Thor asked.

"It's Tabby," Odin said. "Everything has to be a mystery with *fucking-g* Tabby."

I smiled. I loved Odin's accent, the way he pronounced words like *fucking* with an extra syllable: *fucking-g Tabby*.

"Riiiiiight," Thor said.

"Please let it be a shitty security camera photo," I said, sinking down onto the bed next to Odin. "Please, please, please, please!"

Odin slung an arm around my shoulders. "We got this," he said. "Whatever it is, we'll deal with it."

If the photo ZOX had of me was a good one, that would be trouble.

And if ZOX figured out who I was? It's not as if we could take my sisters on the run with us. And what about our farm? Our herd of sheep? Our dog?

Hence my fervent hope that it was a blurry security photo. When it came to identifying a person, a blurry photo was as useless as a kid's crayon drawing.

"Where are we meeting this Tabby?" I asked.

"Guvvey's," Odin said. "It's kind of a nightclub."

"Guvvey's?" I asked.

Odin grinned. "You'll like Guvvey's."

"Or hate it," Thor said.

Chapter Two

WE PARKED IN A NONDESCRIPT DOWNTOWN PARKING garage that stood in a cluster of business district high-rises with mostly dark windows.

"Where is this sort-of-a-nightclub?" I asked as we got out. "Nothing around here even looks open."

"That's the point," Thor said. "You'll see."

"Sooooo mysterioso!"

We took the parking garage elevator to a gloomy basement area and headed down a dark hall and through a door to yet another hall to yet another door.

"What the hell?" I exclaimed.

"Overkill, I know," Thor grumbled.

We finally came to a large, gray door. Odin knocked and gave a password to a camera. He'd ditched the hairy mole, thankfully, as well as the track suit. This weird nightclub had a fancy dress code. We'd had to buy a gown for me to wear at the hotel boutique, and Odin and Thor wore suits.

The lock *clunked* open, and we pushed through and continued. Apparently Guvvey's, being the illegal criminal nightclub it was, had to be shady about everything.

The three of us headed through a dark tunnel, on and on, and then took an elevator up to the 21st floor. We headed to an unmarked door at the end of the hall, or at least I assumed it was a door; I couldn't be sure, being that it had *no doorknob*.

"Are you even kidding me right now?" I asked. "This is like a TV show."

Odin knocked.

A woman with braids and tattoos opened it up and smiled. "Well, well, well, look who's here." She ushered us in to a dark foyer where we were forced to give up our phones.

"You have to give up your phones, but not guns?" I asked.

She flicked her gaze toward Odin.

"She's okay," Odin said. "First time."

She gave me a dark look and let us into a space full of dim, colorful lights and low, pulsating music.

"What?" I protested.

"Give up our guns? You think people like us would dine at a place where we have to give up our guns?" Odin said this like it was the most ridiculous thing ever.

"Yet we gave up our phones. You can't make a call, but it's okay to go on a shooting spree?"

"It's a privacy thing," Thor said. "And to be fair, you can get in a lot of trouble starting a shooting spree."

"Though the windows *are* Plexiglas," Odin added. Like that would be my concern—that the windows wouldn't shatter in the case of free-for-all of gunfire.

Inside, the place was all posh and glam and arty in an ultra-mod way, with blue globe lights and red seating. Apparently the LA criminal element had just as much of a thing for interior design as the LA hotel element did. People sat around low tables; others gathered at the bar. And instead of wallpaper, the walls were plastered floor to ceiling with photographic murals of lions and tigers killing antelopes and rabbits and other prey, images straight off the nature channel, except they were strangely colorized—in pastels, of all things.

I couldn't help but laugh.

"What's so funny?" Odin demanded.

"This art," I said. "That's what's funny."

Thor scowled. He didn't think it was funny.

"Come on, it's funny," I said. "Baby boys like blue trains on their wallpaper, girls get Barbie princess stuff, and wow, you and your crime-happy friends get mammoth, surreal images of predators sinking their teeth into the necks of their helpless prey? And that's not funny?"

"I see it as more Darwinistic than funny," Odin said.

"*Darwinistic*." Thor spat the word. It seemed to bother him, this wallpaper depicting survival of the fittest, a culture of might making right. It made sense, being that he was a doctor by training. He would've taken that doctor's oath to do no harm. In the world of the jungle, Thor would be the one saving the antelope. And really, I would try to save the antelope, too. They seemed sweet and a little bit Bambi-ish, even.

"We're a Darwinistic crowd, baby," Odin said, just as a muscular, tattoo-covered man approached us, laughing.

"No way," the man said, slapping hands with Thor and then Odin. "You boys better have taken the tunnels."

Odin grinned. "We took the tunnels, my friend."

The man tipped up his head by way of answer and led us across the place.

"What does he mean? Isn't everyone supposed to take the tunnels?" I asked Thor.

"He's giving us shit because we have so much heat on us," Thor answered.

As we moved across the room, I noticed how heads turned as we went. The people at the bar watched us. Groups at tables watched us. Even some of the people swaying in the corner to the strange techno music craned their necks around as we passed. It was a strange feeling, to be notorious among the notorious. What's more, everyone was in suits and dresses. The place was a mix of America's sexiest, heavily armed men and women along with lots of menacing and strangely photographic people, also heavily armed, with a few Fellini film extras thrown in.

I tried to act all cool, like I belonged, but I was an antelope—I couldn't get that out of my mind now. Sure, I was an antelope who liked to run up close to the lions and have some big fun, but still. Antelope.

At least Thor was in the antelope camp with me. He would save me if I got bitten.

We were seated at a couch in front of a coffee table that glowed faintly. Everything here was soft with light and color.

A squat woman in a tuxedo walked up with a bottle of scotch. "You fuckers. Still alive. Nice to see you." Thor turned and struck up a conversation with her.

Personally, I was still riveted by the troubling wallpaper. It came to me that Zeus and Odin had once been lions protecting antelopes, but then ZOX, the agency they had dedicated their lives to, turned on them, betrayed them.

That's why they were so into robbing banks—it was their way of *bringing it* to the government agency that wanted them dead because of atrocities they'd witnessed.

They knew too much.

"There she is—over there with the bright white hair." Odin nodded his head at a sturdy-looking woman at the end of the bar with a dyed platinum buzzcut. "She's got her fingers into most of the security cameras in Los Angeles. She's kind of a middleperson, matching buyers and sellers."

Tabby turned toward us right then, as if she sensed our attention. She grabbed her drink and sauntered over, taking the empty seat. "Tabby," she said, holding out her hand.

I shook it. "Isis," I said.

"Got yourself a god name," she said.

I smiled proudly—I couldn't help it. "Yup."

"You can talk in front of her," Odin said, and I sat up a little bit straighter. I felt so lucky, being part of this amazing gang, if only for a little while. "You have the image?"

"Do I have the image?" Tabby asked, like that was outrageous. "It's not so simple as that. What I have is a nervous seller. He works for the company that helps run AV at the fairgrounds."

"How much?" Odin asked.

Tabby shook her head. "Here's what you need to understand: the guy's seriously nervous. The men that grabbed the footage and the image you want to see, they have a lot of juice. He didn't even want me to tell you about him, that's how nervous he is. He'll be mad if you approach him. He'll know it was me who tipped you off, and he might not play ball with me anymore. Which cuts off some of my network."

"It's a sacrifice for you to even give us the name of this guy, that's what you're trying to say to us," Odin clarified.

"That's exactly what I'm trying to say to you," Tabby said. "It'll hurt my business. I'll lose this guy, and that's just for starters."

"Meaning it'll cost us," Thor said.

"Compensation for my loss," Tabby said. "That would be part of the price of this information."

My guys exchanged blank glances, all poker-faced, as usual. Was Tabby really going to suffer if she gave us the name?

Or did she just think my guys were prolific bank robbers with cash coming out their ears? Because that would be very accurate.

Or maybe she sensed how desperate we were. She'd be right about that, too.

We *had* to see that picture.

We had to know the worst.

I had to know.

Odin pulled a card from his pocket, wrote a number on it, and slid it to Tabby. Tabby examined it, crossed out the number, wrote a new one, and passed it back to Odin. Their little dance got repeated one more time, and finally they arrived at a figure that seemed wildly high to me. Thor pulled a wad of bills from his pocket and slapped it on the table, because at Guvvey's, you didn't have to hide when you were doing illegal deals.

Tabby slapped her hand over the pile of money, pulled it toward herself with decisive drama, and counted it. She drove a pretty hard bargain, this Tabby person, and I liked that about her. You didn't get ahead as a woman in the world—and certainly not the criminal world—by being kind and agreeable.

I smiled as she pocketed the money. If and when I had to go back, at least I'd met lots of interesting people. People I barely could've imagined before.

At least I would have that.

Chapter Three

JUST AFTER TEN THAT NIGHT, WE WERE LURKING IN THE entryway of the bland brick apartment building where Tabby's security camera contact, a man named Trevor Olson, lived.

Thor and I were lurking at any rate, pretending to study the mailboxes. Odin was picking the entry door lock. There was a *snick* sound, and the door swung open. We walked in like we owned the place and headed up the stairwell to the fifth floor.

"I hope he's still awake," I said.

"I have a feeling that he'll talk to us either way," Thor said.

"Yes, I have that same feeling," Odin said.

"Now I have that same feeling," I said.

We found the door. Odin knocked.

"Who is it?" somebody—presumably Trevor—yelled from inside.

"We're here on some SunCity business," Odin said.

After a long silence, Trevor said, "Then call the office in the morning."

"It's an urgent piece of business," Odin said.

"So call the 24-hour service line," Trevor said.

"We were referred by Tabby," Odin added.

This got the door open. Trevor was a lanky goth guy wearing sweatpants, a Raiders T-shirt, and a sour-as-lemons scowl. "I don't know any Tabby," he said

Odin lowered his voice. "Tabby certainly knows you."

"You have the wrong person," he said.

"You really want to discuss this out here?" Thor asked in a whisper.

"Go through Tabby. I only talk to Tabby," he said. "This conversation is over."

"You'd rather have it out here in the hall?" Odin asked. "We can have it here in the hall."

Trevor swore and pulled the door open, ushering us in, deciding he'd prefer to have this conversation in a private area. He shut the door and stayed standing. "Out with it, whatever you want. I'm just gonna tell you no."

"The fairgrounds. You have footage that you handed over to a group. We need to see it."

"Definite no on that," Trevor said. "No way."

"We'll pay you well," Odin said.

"I can't," Trevor said. "You're out of luck. Sorry."

Odin strolled over to Trevor's kitchen island and started laying down hundreds.

"I'm gonna fucking strangle Tabby," Trevor added. "You can tell her that. I'm not even supposed to talk about it, and neither is she."

Odin kept going.

"It was really hard to get them a copy," Trevor said. "I can't just get into the hard drive and make another copy without people noticing. There's a whole process to it, and I have to be on site."

Odin turned to him. "But you can give us a look at the footage, can't you?"

Trevor hesitated just enough that even I knew he could let us look if he wanted to. "This conversation is over," he said.

Odin continued to lay down hundreds. So many hundreds.

"I can't," Trevor said, but his eyes were on the money.

"Five thousand," Odin said.

Trevor shook his head. "Even if I wanted to—"

"Just a peek," Thor said. "We don't need copies of the files. Just a peek."

"These people aren't playing," Trevor said.

Odin set down a few more hundreds. "Six large. That's what's behind door number one."

"Door number one," Trevor said.

"That's right," Odin said mysteriously.

Trevor frowned. Was he thinking about door number two? Wondering about it? I sure was.

"Hint," Odin added. "Door number one is the better of the two doors. Vastly preferable."

Trevor frowned at the money.

"I promise you that this group that you fear *didn't* see us come in here, I promise you that—we pay attention to those sorts of things. But let's pretend they did see us. What difference does it make if you show us at this point? Either way, they'll assume you showed us."

Trevor scowled. "I'll explain that I didn't."

"But you're gonna show us." Odin pushed the money toward him. "You may as well take this."

Trevor turned his lemony scowl to Thor, and finally to me.

He scowled at me for an extra-long time.

Did he think my status at the lone woman in the group might give me some moderating influence on badass Odin?

Not likely!

If anything, Odin was a bad influence on me. A *terrible* influence, in fact, leading me down a dark path of crime, overindulgence, and scathingly dirty sex acts.

Best.

Path.

Ever.

Trevor snatched up the money and shoved it into a cigar box. "Stay there." He left the room and came back with a laptop. He sat down and started tapping. "They grabbed a ninety-second clip of an incident—a medical situation at a car show. Some guy collapsed and they carted him off." He cued it up and turned the laptop around to face us.

There he was—Zeus on the floor. The men from ZOX were standing around him, arguing with the paramedics, who quickly backed off. They started loading Zeus onto a stretcher.

Moments later, there I was, pushing my way in, pretending to be a nurse. Odin slowed the playback, isolating the different frames that showed my face. He handed his phone to me. "Take pictures," he said.

"Hey," Trevor said. He wasn't happy about the pictures.

Odin gave him a hard look. "This is happening."

I got shots of each still that showed my face. There were no real high-quality images, but they weren't as shitty and blurry as I'd hoped.

We finished up and headed out and down the stairwell, leaving Trevor and his lemony scowl several thousand bucks richer.

"What do you think?" I asked as we rushed down flight after flight.

"We'll see. I'll run it through my own software. It's not a clear picture, but there are a few good shots. My guess is a forty-percent accuracy."

"Meaning a forty-percent chance they can find me from it?" I asked.

"Yeah, that would be my guess," Odin said. "If they keep hammering at it."

We pushed out the doors into the cool, balmy night and hopped into our car.

"Forty percent doesn't seem like a good thing," I said as Odin navigated the car out into the stream of traffic.

"It's not," he said morosely. "But luckily, my IT skills are a thing of blazing awesomeness, shining like a thousand suns, stupefying my enemies and leaving them gasping in the wind."

"Stupefying them *and* leaving them gasping in the wind?" I teased.

"Both," Odin said resolutely.

I smiled. I loved when he was dramatic like that. Yet another one of the zillion things I'd miss about him.

Thor called Zeus and put him on speaker, updating him on the situation.

"At least we know what we're dealing with," Zeus said. "And I haven't seen anything unusual here."

"How are my sisters?" I asked.

"They're not twirling around in the pastures singing show tunes or anything, but they're getting on with their lives. Vanessa delivered a load of cheese to the Piggly Wiggly today."

"Was it gouda?" I asked.

"I don't know," Zeus said.

"Probably gouda. That batch was going to be ready first." I sat back, watching the streetlights and neon signs whiz by in the darkness. For some reason, I desperately wanted to know what the cheese was. So stupid. I really did miss my sisters. And I missed our dog, Petey. I missed him racing around the pastures. I even missed the sheep, all with their different personalities.

I took solace in the fact that Vanessa, at least, knew I was safe, thanks to the sly message I'd sent her when I ordered one of our very expensive wool comforters. But I knew she'd feel better if I were home.

Not like I'd have a choice.

"It would be either gouda or blue cheese," I said. "Those are our specialties right now. We were thinking about getting into brie, though. Sheep's milk brie."

Thor leaned up from the back seat. "I bet the people of Baylortown love having fresh artisanal cheese in their local grocer," he said.

"Yes, the blazing deliciousness of our cheese shines like a thousand suns, stupefying all rival cheese producers and leaving them gasping in the wind," I said wistfully.

Odin snorted.

Back at the hotel, Odin worked into the night, with breaks now and then to curse the hotel Wi-Fi. I tried to stay up with him, playing soft music and bringing him fizzy waters, but eventually I crashed on the couch.

When I woke up, my guys were at the little breakfast table, feasting on pastries from a cart that had somehow appeared while I was sleeping. Odin still had his nose in his laptop, naturally.

"Why didn't you wake me up?" I asked.

"Seemed like you needed your sleep," Thor said.

"How's it going? Do you feel like you erased me from the internet enough?"

Odin grunted at his screen, deep in do-not-disturb mode.

"Not yet," Thor said, gazing out at the sunrise.

Not yet. No news. Was that good news?

I took a quick shower and pulled myself together as best I could—I didn't want my guys to remember me with bedhead and a face full of smeared makeup. When I came out, Thor had fixed me a coffee.

"So, still working on it?" I asked, taking the small porcelain cup.

They gave each other strange looks.

"What?" I demanded. "Not sure yet?"

Thor's tone was ominous. "I wouldn't say that exactly."

My pulse pounded. "What does that mean?"

"You might want to have a few sips of coffee first," he said.

"What does *that* mean? Because you think I need to be awake for whatever news you have?"

"Yeah," Odin grumbled.

I took a sip. "Am I to assume that the news isn't about your decision to wear kilts for the rest of our time together?"

Neither of them so much as quirked a lip. Seriously not a good sign.

Odin hit a few keys and turned the laptop screen to me. Zeus's face filled the screen. "Good morning," he said.

Chills ran down my spine. "What's going on? Are my sisters okay?"

"Yeah, everyone's fine," Zeus said.

"Sit," Thor said.

"Okay." I sat down on the couch. "Just tell me!"

Thor sucked in a deep breath.

"Oh my god," I whispered. "What?"

Odin came over and sat down next to me. "I'm reasonably sure I got all of the recent pictures," he said. "But there are still some out there, of that I have no doubt. Pictures of you through the years."

My pulse began to race. "Which means we can't stop them from identifying me," I said.

"Not so fast," Zeus piped up from the laptop. "The good news is that facial recognition software has a hard time factoring in age progression. The accuracy goes way down. The bad news is that ZOX has all the time in the world to find you. They could narrow their pool of possible Isis's down to a few thousand and take years to investigate each and every one."

"And they'd do that?" I asked.

"Yeah. Especially the guy assigned to our case—Agent Denko. He's ruthless. The man never sleeps."

"Oh."

Odin gripped my arm. "Here's the good news. The first thing the ZOX analysts will do is exclude people who were dead at the time that the photo was taken. Massive waste of time for dead people to show up in the final results."

"How is that good news?" I asked. "I wasn't dead at the time."

"But what if you *had* been dead at the time?"

"Is this why I needed coffee? Are we getting into parallel timelines?"

"Not actually dead, but what if people believed you'd died beforehand?"

It took me a while to comprehend all of this. "So...fake my death? Retroactively?"

"*Melinda's* death, not Isis's," Zeus said from the laptop.

Thor said, "We'd fake the death of Melinda, the hostage we took. We'd arrange it so that your long-dead body turns up. It would be convincing."

"How?"

They outlined their plan.

I listened in stunned silence.

Apparently Zeus's CIA contact had access to a burnt female corpse with the right characteristics to pass for dead Melinda. Whoever this was, she'd been shot while sitting in a car in the desert, and then her car had been set on fire. The estimated time of death was a week before Zeus and I had been captured.

Zeus had already broken into my dentist's computer records, guessing correctly that I went to the only dentist in Baylortown. He'd passed my records to the CIA guy, who was already modifying the dental X-rays of the corpse to match up.

"I don't know about this. I mean, let my sisters think I got shot and burned to death in the desert? I don't know if I can do that."

Zeus swore under his breath.

Not okay with this plan.

Odin focused grimly on something out the window.

Thor regarded me sadly.

Right.

There *wasn't* a choice. I was in the same position as Venus—I could never go home again.

"I get it," I said.

"We never wanted you to be forced into staying," Thor said.

"I know," I said. "It's okay."

"No, it's not," Zeus growled. "It's not at *all* okay."

"But I want to stay," I said. "You know I do. And I'm the one who got involved when you told me to disappear. I share the blame on this. It's just...how can I put them through believing...how could I do that to them?"

Nobody said anything.

Thor settled onto the couch on the other side of me and set a gentle hand on my shoulder.

"I mean, a burnt corpse?" I said. "There has to be another way. Maybe we let them know it's fake?"

"It has to be real to them," Zeus said. "There's so much media involved with your disappearance, so many cops and detectives sniffing around. Your sisters have to think it's real. They can't be playacting."

"But maybe after?" I tried.

"The truth puts them in danger," Thor said. "Your sisters are young. Do you really want to ask them to keep a secret that puts them in the position of aiding and abetting internationally wanted fugitives? Not to mention the danger from ZOX if one of them slipped up?"

This was happening too fast. Staying with the guys is what I'd wanted—desperately—but not like this.

"I'd never be able to see them again," I said.

"Never's a long time," Odin said. "Never say never."

"But it's what we're looking at right now," I said numbly.

Nobody said anything. We all knew it was true.

Could I do it?

But I didn't have a choice, now. "Wait, could I keep buying the Paris Hilton quilts?" I asked. "And leaving little messages? It would give them hope. Like maybe, just maybe—"

"This is not a game," Zeus barked. "You can't be sending them messages."

"We can keep buying the quilts once in a while. But no more messages," Odin said. "At least for the foreseeable future."

"Okay," I said. "No, I get it."

Thor straightened my bathrobe lapels. "How are you doing?"

Conflicting feelings swirled through me. I didn't want to leave my guys, but how could I never see my sisters again? How could I cause them such pain?

"I know it's not what you want," Zeus said darkly.

"I want to stay here—that part's not the question."

"Saying you want to stay and being *forced* to stay are two very different things," Zeus said. "Nobody wants to be told they can never go home again."

Zeus was talking about himself as much as me—I knew that deep in my bones.

And there was something else I knew deep in my bones.

I stood and gave Zeus a long, hard look, and then Odin, and then Thor.

"I need you guys to hear this once and for all. If door number one is staying here and never seeing my sisters again and door number two is everything going back the way it was—I stay back at the farm, never knowing you all, never knowing this life, you know what door I'd pick? Can you guess?"

Thor sucked in a silent breath. Zeus watched me slow and steady. Odin pressed his hands together, waiting.

They needed to hear it from me.

"I'd pick door number one. This door. The one we're walking through. I'd pick it over and over."

Zeus said nothing, but I could feel his relief like a physical thing—the weight of it, the gravity of it.

Odin's eyes sparkled.

"For real?" Thor asked hopefully.

"Every day of the week," I whispered.

"You'll miss them," Thor said.

"You'll help me," I said. "We'll all help each other."

Zeus gave me a wary look, still unsure.

Odin crossed his legs and sat back like an elegant man of

leisure. "It's natural to want to stay, of course. After a couple days with us, what woman wouldn't want to choose this? We live in the most luxury. We give the most *fucking-g* pleasure."

"We have skills," Thor said. "As you know. Utterly unmatched."

"Plus, humility." I leaned back on Thor's shoulder, enjoying being in this illegal nest with my Peter Pans.

Odin scowled. "And you'll have to continue to obey our rules and perform the duties."

I smiled. "Would the duties be erotic?"

"Very," Thor whispered.

"And the punishment would be severe, yet exquisite," Odin said.

"So we kill Melinda," I said. "And maybe we can find a way to fix this thing in the end. You can't live your lives as bank robbers forever. It's not who you are."

Zeus's gaze went diamond-hard. "You think we haven't tried to fix this thing? There are some problems you can't solve."

I bit my tongue. Even the vague hope of changing his circumstances seemed to annoy him.

And he still wasn't sure of me. He was still stung from Venus, and one night of weird role-playing while roasting in a railcar hadn't changed that.

Right then and there, I vowed to prove myself to him. To all of them.

They thought I was just a farm girl, but we were in this together. Maybe we could get out of it together.

Maybe we could all go home.

Thor turned my face to his and kissed me. Odin smiled his devilish smile.

Chapter Four

"Eep!" I cried.

Zeus tightened his grip on my calf and gave me one of his green-eyed glowers that always made my insides melt. "Don't be a baby," he growled in a way that was probably supposed to sound stern but was mostly sexy.

We were in a new hotel—the five-star Hotel Casa Del Sol—that had gorgeous ocean views out of huge arched windows. We'd spent the morning feasting, and then we'd walked the beach in glam disguises, discussing a bank my guys wanted to rob: the First West.

Now we were back in the room, and I was getting the gang tattoo.

I was sitting on the couch next to Thor with my leg up on the coffee table; it was Zeus's job to hold it still while Odin worked on my ankle tattoo.

I'd never gotten a tattoo before. I didn't know it was needles!

"If you would stop squirming, it would be over sooner," Zeus added.

I plopped my head back on the couch cushion and stared at the posh ceiling. I distracted myself with thoughts of how grand hotels think of everything—posh ceilings, mints, guys in top hats to open doors.

I liked top hats, but my guys refused to wear them when I asked last week. No amount of sexy enticing would change that. I really wanted to have my guys in top hats, but not as badly as I wanted to have them in kilts.

Have them in kilts, meaning in the fashion sense *and* the carnal sense.

Thor looked at me sadly. "It *is* one of the most sensitive parts of the body," he said. "But if we knocked you out, it wouldn't mean as much."

"Eep!" I said, as the sting of the tattoo needle intensified.

I squeezed my eyes shut. Should I say *Mississippi*? My safe word?

Zeus snorted. "If you say *eep* one more time, I swear, Odin is going to start all over again. On the other ankle."

I stared at the chandelier as Odin's implement vibrated its painful little path along the tender inside of my ankle. More needling. And more.

"Eep!" I whispered under my breath.

The needling stopped.

Odin stood and scowled at me through his black wavy hair. "I'm gonna screw it up if you don't behave. Do you want your gang tattoo to look like it was done by a third grader?"

"No," I said. "I guess."

Odin shook his head. His glasses and the bruising around his eye from a recent scuffle almost cancelled out his pretty boy looks —*almost*. "You usually like a little pain, Isis."

True. But not this kind!

I didn't know what was wrong with me. I felt proud to be getting the tattoo of our bank-robbing gang—an angry cloud with four fierce lightning bolts. Before I joined up, the design featured only three lightning bolts. The last bolt would represent me.

Odin sat back down and dabbed at my ankle.

"Here's the thing," I said. "What if the cops caught me and recognized the tattoo, and I cracked and led them to you?" I was joking a little, but a little bit not.

Zeus gazed at me with extra smoldering intensity. His nut-brown hair was still wet from a recent shower. I wanted to touch it. I wanted to touch *him*, just run my hands over his stubbly cheek. "The cops'll catch us when we're dead," he growled.

My mouth went dry; I so loved when he talked tough like that. Still, I worried. "What if I'm the weak link?"

"The tattoo isn't about that. It's about family," Zeus said. "It says we belong together."

"Seriously, though, what if I screw it up for all of us?" What I was really asking was, *what if I'm not worthy?*

Zeus stood and came around the coffee table. He sat down next to me on the arm of the couch. "Listen to me, Isis." He set his hands gently on the sides of my neck, fingers lightly touching my ears. "We're a family now. You know what family means? We get to mess things up and be messed up, and we still belong together. You won't be rid of us, even if you act like the biggest screw-up in the world. And vice versa."

"So sweet." I was acting all cool to cover my strong emotions, but in truth, I felt my eyes misting up. These guys meant every-thing to me.

"I know you can never go home again," he continued, "and part of that is our fault."

I started to protest—I'd made my own choices.

He waved it off. "I know you miss your sisters. But we're family now, Ice. We're here for you. But if you don't want the tattoo, you don't have to get it."

"It's not that I don't want the tattoo. I want it. And you know I'm a hundred percent into this."

Thor smoothed a bit of hair from my forehead. Even my hair was different in this life—short and platinum blonde instead of long and red. "Good, because we're a hundred percent into you. Actually, we're three hundred percent into you."

I grinned. "I don't know that we've gotten quite that far yet in our relationship."

Thor smiled devilishly and crossed his lanky legs. "The night's still young, baby."

Shivers ran over my skin.

"And, also, I think you're three hundred percent into our gang rules," Thor said.

My belly tightened. Yes, I liked the dirty rules.

Thor said, "Actually, I think you joined entirely for the rules. And correct me if I'm wrong, but I do believe the rules state that we can use your body in whatever way we see fit to satisfy our each and every carnal desire. Which would include tattooing you however and wherever we please."

"Correction," I said. "I didn't join for the rules that let you use my body to satisfy your carnal desires. I joined as a hostage. I *stayed* for the dirty rules."

Odin fixed me with a hard look. "Why ever you're here and why ever you stay, this tattoo says we'll never leave you behind, no matter what."

"And you'll never leave us behind," Thor added softly.

There it was.

"I would never," I said quickly. *Never leave you the way she did* —that was the subtext.

"We know," Thor said.

Did they, though? My roguish criminals were a little bit vulnerable. They'd committed to Venus, and the three of them were hurt and grief-stricken when she killed herself.

Letting me join was a risky act for them—as risky as the most daring bank takeover. You could say they didn't have a choice in the matter, but it was still risky. I wanted to rise to the occasion, to be worthy of their belief in me.

"Let's do this," I said. "Together forever."

Zeus came to me, then. He grabbed my hair and pressed a kiss to my forehead.

I closed my eyes, loving it.

I said it again. "Let's do it."

"Good," Odin said. "Because God Pack membership is not the stuff of a *fucking-g* pinky shake."

I looked over Odin's shoulder at the vase of tulips on the side table—flowers Zeus would've ripped up not too long ago, but in the few weeks since we'd almost died in that railcar, he hadn't done it once. It was as if he'd worked out something that needed working out.

I felt this surge of affection for my bandits. We'd come through a lot in a short time. And we had a code. Sure, our code was all about being a gang of criminals living dissipated, sex-crazed lives in luxury hotels, but it was our code. We were our own goddamn family. I felt so proud. And I wanted the tattoo.

"Naturally, it's the most intricate tattoo known to humankind," I said. "I think this thing has a higher level of detail than a dollar bill. You guys only got one angry lightning bolt added today. I have to get the whole outrageous thing."

"The lightning bolt is not angry, it's wrathful," Odin corrected. "Wrath is more constructive than anger."

"And cooler," Thor added. "Wrath is cooler than anger."

"Do it." I shoved my foot back across the coffee table at Odin. He watched me, all hot and scowly, toying with the tattoo implement. He'd once told me he'd gotten his looks from ancestors in the Berber tribe of North Africa. He was proud of his heritage, but he hated being so gorgeous—it detracted from his image as a dangerous criminal. The things he did to counteract his looks— the two-day beard, the messy hair, the dorky outfits—it just intensified his handsomeness. I didn't have the heart to tell him.

He turned the thing back on.

I winced.

He turned it off. "I haven't even touched you yet. I cannot

work like this." Odin set the thing down, removed his glasses, and stood, stretching his fingers. "Isis, I recall you becoming quite wantonly aroused by certain kinds of pain. I recall a certain afternoon—"

"That's different," I interrupted.

Odin smiled his gorgeous smile. "Our innocent sheep farmer, writhing in ecstasy under a man's firm hand coming down over her soft, fleshy buttocks. I recall a certain sheep farmer begging for more—"

"Stop..." I felt my face heat.

I looked over at Thor, who suppressed a grin, but I saw it in his blue eyes. His gaze traveled down to my neck, my chest. My chest would be pink under my shirt. He loved to tease me that I was a sex maniac. Maybe I was.

"Excuse me if it's different when it's, you know, exciting and sexy instead of just...abject torture."

"That's context, nothing more." Odin flung a hand at me. "Strip her clothes off and tie her to the coffee table."

My pussy tingled. "Excuse me?" I said. "Tie me up while I'm getting my tattoo?"

"Do it," Odin said, wiping his tattoo gun. "You need a new context."

"Good idea." Thor let loose his grin.

"Sooooo...hold on!" My blood raced with excitement.

"You want her on her back or stomach?" Thor asked.

"Back," Odin said. "Strip her and strap her. While I still feel inspired."

The command turned my legs to jelly. This tattoo operation was starting to look up.

Zeus gazed over me, a glint of danger in his green eyes. "Get up, Ice."

I met his gaze. The day they robbed the bank they wore zombie masks, but even then, his eyes mesmerized me.

"Will you disobey, Isis?" Zeus asked. "Is that what I'm seeing?"

Slowly, I stood, feeling naked already, unsure what they were planning. What could possibly distract me from poking needles? But I loved following their commands...almost as much as I loved resisting them.

Zeus stood almost a foot taller than me, all brutish beauty. In the world of gods, Zeus was an alpha. Within the gang, he was definitely the leader. He touched a finger to the bottom of my chin. "Strip her, Thor."

Bright shivers cascaded over me as Thor's arms slipped around me from behind, unbuckling my belt. The way Zeus watched my eyes...you could barely call it watching. It was more like he was using his hypnotic gaze to hold me and interrogate me and fuck me all at once.

So alpha hole.

So sexy.

Thor fumbled with the fly of my shorts more than he had to, which amounted to some slyly sexy scrabbling between my legs, and then he slid his fingers down between my legs, intensifying the heat there. I closed my eyes, feverish with excitement, as he pressed his body against mine from behind. Sometimes I still couldn't believe that these sexy, fabulous bandits who took their names from gods and comic book heroes and wanted me and me alone.

"Keep looking at me," Zeus grated.

I opened my eyes.

Zeus said, "We will distract you so thoroughly, Isis, that tattoo needle will feel like a summer breeze."

Thor nuzzled my ear. "You might even get into it." He pushed my shorts down over my hips as Zeus watched.

Warmth pulsed through my core.

"Isis loves a good distraction, don't you, Isis?" Odin said.

"So what's that exactly supposed to mean?" I asked.

"You'll see," Zeus growled.

"I think we'll need to collect all the belts and scarves in this whole place, though," Thor said.

"I don't really see how this is going to work—"

My protests dissolved as Zeus grabbed the collar of my tank top and ripped it right down the middle.

I gasped.

"You don't need to see," he said. "Probably best you don't."

Eep!

I leaned back against Thor, blood racing. I trusted my bandits—anything could happen with us, and I knew I'd always be cherished. Safe. At least when we were alone together, inside our hotel rooms, we were safe. Out there with them robbing banks...that was scary, even with Zeus and Odin being highly trained military operatives.

You're not immortal. You're not magic. I'd said that to Zeus recently, and he'd assured me they were close—beyond Navy SEALS, beyond elite, beyond secret.

Zeus caressed the tender flesh of my breasts with his rough fingers. "I love it when you don't wear a bra," he said. He took my hand, kissed my fingers. "You're learning our preferences."

"Actually, I'm down to one favorite bra. And considering you love ripping my clothes? That bra is officially reserved for restaurants and robberies."

Thor said, "We're rich bank robbers. We'll buy another bra."

"Actually, we're running out of money," Odin said from his stool across the coffee table. "Now hurry the fuck up."

"Wait, what?" Thor asked.

Odin examined his tattoo instrument. I got the feeling he was hiding something. Was it bad news? Something more than money? "Belts, scarves, ties," Odin said, looking up with resolve. "First things first."

I stepped out of my shorts and panties as Thor walked off on his dirty scavenger hunt.

I stood there quivering, naked under Zeus's hungry-bear gaze.

Zeus made you vulnerable with that gaze.

And oh, how I wanted him.

Chapter Five

W ITH ONE SLOW, DELIBERATE MOTION, Z EUS POINTED
to the coffee table, just pointed at it.

He always wore a simple ring on his large hand, something
Celtic. He'd always seemed quite Irish to me—Irish and feral with
creamy skin and hard eyes.

His voice was a low rumble. "Lie down. On your back."

Heat licked up my spine as I stretched myself out onto the
coffee table like an offering on an altar. The surface felt cool and
hard under my shoulder blades and my bare ass. I squeezed my legs
together.

Everything about my hot bank robbers turned me on—their
naughty orders, their brutish attentions. It was like I'd stumbled
into a Disney World of dangerous sex fantasies.

This was a whole new ride now—the tattoo distraction ride,
definitely a scary one, with a dark tunnel leading to thrills.

Odin bent over me, placing a hand next to my hip, amber eyes
glinting. "We'll get this thing done now."

He kissed my belly, and then my belly button. I moaned and
shoved my hands into his thick, moppy hair.

"Maybe we can forget about the tattoo situation altogether," I teased, just to get him going. In truth, I really did want the tattoo. "Maybe we can go with temporary tattoos."

"No chance." He kissed downward along my neatly trimmed pubes. "Oh, this won't do." He grabbed my knees, pulled them apart, and kissed my heated sex.

I sucked in a breath. I wondered vaguely if this tattoo bit could maybe stretch into a multi-day process.

"Slide down. Knees over the edge."

Heat bloomed between my legs as I slid down.

I felt Odin position my right foot on something—the footstool, I guessed—which raised my knee slightly above the table. "Give me that rope, Zeus," Odin said.

Zeus threw Odin his belt and Odin leashed my foot to the stool, making it into a giant platform shoe. Or a stilt for a dirty, dirty stilt walker.

"Your tattoo will be *fucking-g* exquisite," Odin said. "If you would only hold still. We're nearly halfway done."

Thor returned with a bunch of belts and scarves. Zeus used a black sequined scarf to tie my left calf securely to the other table leg so that my legs were splayed apart. Just lying there like that, one knee up, exposed and waiting, cool air on my pussy, was exhilarating.

I felt like I was on top of a ski jump or a roller coaster in the moment before the plunge—the delicious point where you are about to give yourself over to a powerful force you can't control.

Zeus sat next to me on the coffee table. I said a silent thanks to the hotel gods that this coffee table was metal—we'd accidentally broken a bit of hotel furniture over the past weeks, and apparently it cost a lot of money to replace that stuff.

What was that Odin said about running out of money?

Zeus rested his heavy hand on my belly. "How to distract our squirmy goddess..." Calloused fingers slid down to my crotch.

I lifted my hips, pushing into his touch.

"God, you're wet," he said.

"I've been deprived lately."

Odin tied my knee to the corner of the table.

"I've been deprived, too, it just so happens." He dragged his finger lazily through my cleft. "And I haven't even begun to sate myself on you."

I shivered with pleasure as he gazed down at me, touched me again, lightly, lazily, teasing me.

"Please sate," I gasped. "Sate more."

Zeus had lushly expressive lips. They were beautiful when he smiled and wicked when he frowned. Right now he was twisting them, a dark and playful look of his that could look a little bit cruel.

In a hot way.

"Maybe it's sating me to drive you half mad," he whispered, as he drew his finger further up my sex and over my pubic bone. Up, up, up to my belly went his finger, leaving my needy and aching clit behind.

Noooo!

I stilled his hands, pushed them back downward. "Reverse course," I gasped, pushing at his arm. "You must reverse course."

"Oh, dear," he said. "Hand me two scarves and the handcuffs, Thor."

Gulp.

"Apparently tying you up won't be enough. Do you know what Thor has to go and get now?" He glanced at Thor significantly.

"I have an idea," I said, thinking more restraints. Hopefully rough-textured ropes.

"I doubt that," Thor said as he left the room.

Zeus ran a belt under the coffee table and buckled it around my middle, right at my belly button. He crisscrossed a long scarf over my chest, like an X between my breasts. Then he took out the cushy cuffs, all plush inside and Velcro on the outsides and strong as hell.

"Hands behind your head. Fingers knit. Now." Zeus spoke like a commander. His military background was as useful during sexual escapades as it was in robberies.

"I can't believe you're tying my hands, too. For a tattoo?"

"Was that a *Mississippi*?" He lowered his voice. "Do it."

His tone was a bolt through my belly.

Breathlessly, I complied, placing my hands as he instructed. He velcroed cuffs around my wrists and tied restraints under the table. I imagined the long straps crisscrossed under there. Why my hands?

"I can be distracted with my hands free, you know."

Another belt. I'd never been tied up so thoroughly. I wiggled a little, just to test.

"No, you must not move." Odin ran a fingernail down my calf. "It is only this, only sensation."

I gasped. *Only.*

I lay there, as still as could be. The only part of me that could move at this point were the butterflies fluttering wildly in my belly.

"If they do not hurry, I'm going to lose my *fucking-g inspiration*," Odin said.

"You never lose your inspiration," I said.

He kissed my knee. Like that was his answer.

Odin was the group techie and also the group tattoo artist. He'd had practice in an Algerian prison, as it turned out, but oddly, had never himself gotten a tattoo until the one for our gang. It was the one tattoo he knew he'd want to keep until death. "If you move, you will have squiggles instead of proud *fucking-g* bolts."

I waited there, cool and vulnerable in my nakedness and filled with a sweet apprehension I'd come to know well in my short time with the gang.

Were they making me wait in order to stoke my excitement? Did they not understand how unbearably excited I felt?

Zeus leaned in. "How does it feel?"

"Like I'm about to be roasted on a spit," I panted.

"Oh, we have something hotter, Isis." Zeus trailed a finger through my throbbing sex, paused, and circled around my tender nub. My belly undulated to the sweet feeling. Odin kissed my toe at the same time and then sucked it.

"Oh wow," I breathed. "The tattooing does feel better now."

Zeus drew his hand away again. I gasped at the loss. I was right on the verge.

Thor came back into the room. He wore his longish blond hair slicked back. With his lanky, athletic body, he looked like a Swedish tennis player, and he had a wicked look on his face.

"What now?" I asked.

He leaned down to kiss me, brushing a finger over my nipple, which drew tight at his touch. "You are always so responsive when you're tied down," he observed.

True enough!

I pulled at the cuffs above and behind my head.

The plush velvet inside them felt warm and soft.

Zeus's hand on my belly felt deliciously heavy. He was such a tease, to rest his hand there, doing nothing. Well, actually he was doing something—he was demonstrating his command over me. He'd touch me when he damn well felt like it, and I could do nothing about it, tied as I was.

Eep!

"But would it be better to *not* be responsive when you're getting a tattoo?" I teased.

"Unless the pain is balanced," Thor said.

"With pleasure?" I asked hopefully.

"Well..." Thor looked like he was thinking about that.

"*Well*?" I demanded.

"Do you trust me, Isis?" Thor asked. "Have I ever endangered or upset you?"

I thought about a certain joyride we'd taken in Kansas City. "Ummm..."

Zeus chose this moment to move his hand back down between my legs, and I blew out a breath I'd been holding. He rubbed my clit with the flat of his finger.

"Omigod," I said.

Odin grabbed my ankle again and blotted my tattoo.

"I don't know if I'm ready for more tattoo," I said.

Thor whispered, "That will be the least of your concerns." The next thing I knew, he was tying a blindfold around my head, covering my eyes.

"Really?" I said. "I can't even..." But Zeus was stroking my clit in a new way, and I gave myself over to that sensation of his fingers on the wet, vulnerable lips between my legs.

Thor closed his lips over my nipple, sending quivers of pleasure through me.

"Omigod," I said again. "I for sure won't be still if I orgasm."

"Don't orgasm, then," Zeus said.

Thor tweaked my nipples between his fingers—at least I think it was Thor. All I knew was that there were warm fingers stroking between my legs and cool fingers rubbing my nipples into diamond-like hardness. It was a sex Hootenanny!

I was still bracing for Odin to start drilling my ankle.

Until I felt the bite on my nipple.

"Hey!" Mad sensation radiated through me, filling my head, not letting up. I couldn't see with the blindfold, but I assumed it was Thor, clutching my nipple in his teeth.

The strange pain of it felt exciting—especially combined with Zeus's highly pleasurable stroking. Sharp and soft, like salt with chocolate. Thor's teeth at my nipple were the salt, Zeus's fingers stroking through my sensitive folds was the chocolate.

"Oh, yesssss," I said, getting way too into it. I was so into it I barely noticed the stingy needles at my foot. Something cool and light was laid on my chest. Like a little chain.

Then Thor bit my other breast, at the same time. I began to pant.

Wait, that was impossible. It had to be Zeus biting a nipple at the exact same time as Thor...*with identical pressure and orientation, while stroking my sex.* Like some kind of next-level multi-tasking.

"Oh, wow," I gasped.

All these points of feeling were doing something funny to my body, drowning each other out, like competing music in the electronics aisle at Target. But unlike the cacophony of the electronics aisle, these feelings were a luscious symphony.

"Wow," I panted. "Synchronized biting."

Zeus chuckled. "Not *exactly*."

Thor snorted. "Yeah, not quite."

Wait, how were they talking with their teeth on my nipples? My mind was being blown with both pleasure and logistics now...until it came to me that it wasn't their teeth on my nipples.

"What? Nipple clamps?" I pulled at my handcuffs which intensified the feeling in my nipples. I sucked in a breath.

"You were just enjoying it," Thor said.

"Til I knew what it was," I panted.

"Go with it," Zeus commanded.

"You want them off?" Thor asked.

"Um..." I breathed. I wasn't so sure I wanted them off.

"They're not even tight," Thor said.

It was true. They were perfectly bitey in a most enjoyable way.

"And there's a little chain between them. Can you imagine what happens when I pull on it?" I felt him scoop up the little chain. I trembled with anticipation. "Answer. Can you?" Thor whispered in my ear.

Could I imagine? I could very much imagine it. I could very scathingly imagine it.

I felt a tug. The pleasure sharpened.

"Oh," I gasped.

"Now you don't have to imagine, Isis. Every time you

complain or bellyache, I pull the chain. But harder, got it? Say yes. Say you understand."

"Harder?" My mind felt melty.

Thor said, "Got it?"

The needly prickling in my foot continued on, but I hardly cared. There was more drama on my nipples! It was like I'd moved to the far side of stimulation. The smutty land of the midnight sun.

"You're not even paying attention," Thor seethed "Say, *Yes, Thor.*"

"Yes, Thor," I breathed.

"And, if you move your foot at all, we'll tighten them. They're on the lowest setting, but they can go tighter." Thor's fingers shoved into the hair above my blindfold, and I felt his warm breath invade my ear. "Feel it, get into it." I felt his fingers on the fleshy underside of my breast and his warm tongue on my nipple.

As he tongued me, the strange pressure on my nipples seemed to evolve. My mind didn't know what to do with it. The feeling seemed to radiate outward in sparkly waves from my nipples. I was keenly aware of every belt and scarf holding me down, and every time I breathed, my belly seemed to fill with butterflies. And somehow, strangely, the tattooing felt wonderful, too. How was this happening?

I pressed my pelvis upward into Zeus's hand.

"Hey!" Someone yanked on the chain, tugging my nipples outward.

The yank was a blast of intensity sending heat down between my legs; it shocked me more than anything.

"That wasn't a complaint," I protested.

"It was a complaint that Zeus wasn't doing you hard enough," Thor said.

"Movement isn't a complaint," I said.

Another yank.

"Ah!"

One of the clamps tightened. I felt light, nearly weightless, zoning out on the strange bliss of it all.

The tattoo needle was reaching the part of my foot that had hurt the most before, but this time it wasn't pain or pleasure; somehow, contained both. It was like a flower, with pain in the center, and sharp ecstasy ruffling out in wild petals.

I felt Zeus's fingers enter me, two fingers, curling ever so slightly inside me. I wanted to cry tears of joy—I so needed release, so craved it.

Out, then in.

Yessssss.

I knew I wasn't moving, yet I felt like I was whirling a million miles an hour into a pit of pleasure. Needles sparked across my tender ankle and I didn't even care. I just wanted more. More, more, more.

I felt something soft and warm on my right nipple—a tongue, just above where the clamp clamped. "Oh, yes," I gasped.

"You like the new context?" Zeus asked.

"The new context is really great."

Odin grunted in agreement.

Zeus pushed his fingers into me again, rubbing my clit.

"Oh, god, that's too much context!" I said. "I don't think I can hold out!"

Nipple tug. Shivers. Gasp. It was a miracle that I didn't go over the edge right then and there.

"You have to hold out," Zeus said. "Because once Odin is done, I am going to fuck you right on that table."

I panted even harder as I felt Thor's warm breath on my ear. Somewhere along the line, my bandits had discovered the extreme sensitivity of my ears, a discovery they exploited the hell out of.

I tried to keep from orgasming by concentrating on sheep breeds, trying to name as many as possible—there was the Merino, the sweet Texel sheep, the Suffolk, the super-cute Valais blacknose.

"Hey," Thor said as soon as I hit Romanov. "Are you naming sheep breeds?"

"Welllllll," I said.

"Stop. No more sheep breeds. Give yourself over to us. Give us everything, Ice, including your attention. We own you right now."

Heat pulsed through my center.

"No sheep breed naming," he whispered.

It was true—they owned me, just as gravity owned me. I would always fall toward these men.

As if I wasn't close enough to the edge, Thor launched into some blisteringly dirty talk about my total helplessness and various erotic things he had in mind, including dirty alternate uses for the nipple clamps. I could imagine the mischief in his eyes, knowing he was pushing me over. Just the tone of his voice turned me on.

I wondered how long I could keep from plunging into an orgasm.

"Omigod, the talking," I begged. "I can't..."

"You will." He continued on with his dirty talk, but a few moments later, the buzzing and prickling at my foot ceased.

"Done."

Already?

I felt my ankle being blotted. I gasped as somebody unclamped my nipples, and Zeus's fingers were suddenly gone.

A warm torso covered mine. Make that a warm and *massive* torso.

Zeus.

"Oh, yeah," I breathed. The tattoo viewing could wait. "Yes... please!" I writhed underneath the wonderful weight of him. He kissed me, sliding a hand up and down the tender underside of my arm.

He lifted off. I heard a zipper. The rip of a foil package. Heavy, rough hands on my thighs. A tongue between my legs. He licked me again and again, torturing me softly. My arousal spiked with every drag of his tongue.

Finally I felt his forearms come down on the table outside my shoulders, caging me, felt his lips close over one exquisitely tingly, puffy-feeling nipple. I gasped as he licked and kissed. With the clamps off, my nipples were like Fourth of July sparklers, going wild with feeling. It was almost too much pleasure.

Key word: *almost*.

I would definitely be moving my initials over to the pro-nipple-clamp column now.

I felt his stomach move against my belly, and I writhed under him to feel more, wishing my wrists weren't tied, yet quite pleased they were. I loved being helpless under Zeus.

His hands roved possessively over my deliciously immobilized self. I wasn't sure if I could last—I might come before he was even inside me. Especially when I realized Odin and Thor were likely watching Zeus take me brutishly.

The idea of a watcher or two—not participating, but just watching—thrilled me to no end.

Zeus moved one of his arms off the table. I felt a hand at my sex and the sensation of him filling me, pushing into me. I gasped at the perfect feeling of it. Zeus drove into me fully then, filling me firmly, sending me into oblivion. He moaned softly with every thrust, *uh, uh, uh...* a Zeus signature I'd come to love. I felt lulled by the rhythm of his pleasure, pleasured by his pleasure. It was the *uh-uh* that sent me over.

"I have to..."

"Come, goddess, come," he panted, sounding half out of his mind. "Take your fill." He bit my earlobe and thrust into me harder as I shattered apart with a cry, my orgasm lifting me in waves that gave way to larger waves, breaking and crashing over me.

Something scraped my neck—his teeth. I hoped they'd made a mark. I wanted to be claimed and consumed and marked in every way by my bandits.

Zeus groaned one last time, louder and gruffer than the last, and stilled inside me. I felt only the vibration of his cock in me.

"Oh," he said softly. "Fuck." He cupped my cheeks with his hands and kissed me, resting still on me. I knew he was half supporting himself, but I loved the feel of the weight he was giving me. I kind of wanted him to crush me. I could never get enough. I couldn't wait to see my new tattoo.

Chapter Six

"Ice," Zeus said, pulling off my blindfold. He stayed in me. We watched each other, and something that felt like honesty passed between us. Sometimes, with my bandits, I felt like I was home, but at the same time, like we were all careening out of control.

Two rips of Velcro later, I was sitting up. Thor threw me a warm, damp washcloth from across the room. I just barely caught it. He threw one to Zeus.

"Hurry up, but don't look at your tattoo yet," Odin commanded.

Zeus lifted his green gaze to me. "That was…" He kissed me and drew the warm cloth over my crotch. "Completely and totally sating. One of the most freaking sating experiences I've ever had."

"Sating doesn't even cover it," I said.

"Too true." He cast the cloth aside and knelt by my feet, undoing the belt and the tie. His fingers seemed to tremble as they grazed the top of the piece of plastic wrap Odin had put on my tattoo to protect it.

He undid the belts and scarves. Then he lifted his gaze to me, and my breath caught at the emotion on his face.

What had struck such emotion into him? What was different?

Then I realized: it was the tattoo.

The tattoo meant big things to Zeus, maybe to all three of my guys. Like we were in a gangster marriage. So sweet.

The fluidity with which they moved between tough-guy criminals and lost boys sometimes shocked me, but I loved it.

A lot.

And I loved how emotional they could become.

I slid to the edge and pulled him to me, held his head against my stomach. I loved everything about these guys. I needed them in a way I couldn't describe.

Odin and Thor sat over at the dining table in their hotel robes. Had they been in the hot tub? How long had Zeus and I been fucking?

I ruffled Zeus's hair, then I grabbed my own robe off the couch. As a gang, we were heavy into wearing the hotel robes. In fact, the plushness of hotel robes seemed to be one of the criteria by which they evaluated fancy hotels. My bank robbers had a kind of overheated lifestyle. They pulled big jobs and then blew all the money on outrageously priced suites in outrageously priced hotels —and fabulous room service meals, too.

No complaints here!

Zeus disappeared across the suite into one of the bathrooms that this hotel called a spa. Yes, it was that kind of place.

I stood up, feeling a bit wobbly. "I think I need a health shake or something," I said.

Thor strolled over with a glass of champagne. "Try some 1990 Perrier Jouët."

I grinned. "I guess it'll have to do." I took the glass from Thor and let him guide me to the table, which was laid out with fruits and cheeses, our favorite evening meal.

Odin stood eyeing me. "I am a genius, you know." He swigged a glass of scotch.

"We know," Thor said.

"A tattoo under those conditions?" he said. "Nearly impossible."

"I was doing great!" I protested.

"Debatable," Odin said, raising an eyebrow. "To imagine that a girl who so longs for the feel of a man's firm hand on her ass could be such a baby."

"Stop it!" I laughed. "God!"

"Stop teasing Isis." Thor draped himself over a chair, one arm over the back, one leg over the armrest. He reached over and grabbed the grapes and held them above his upturned face, feeding himself, looking every inch the decadent god.

"This is excellent gouda," Odin said. "I believe even the cheese-head farmer would agree." His tone was joking, but something was bugging him, I could tell.

I grabbed a slice and tried it. The gouda sparked with flavor. "Pretty good. Almost as good as Sunny Sisters sheep gouda. But not quite."

Odin smiled. He liked that. He was all about the boasting.

I gazed out the window, scanning the beach. Way down to the left you could see the Santa Monica pier, and beyond it, an impossibly blue ocean under a fiery sunset. It made me dizzy that this view was something I was seeing in real life and not a postcard.

I wished my sisters could see it—none of us had ever been out of Wisconsin before.

And I couldn't go home again.

It was still hard to get used to.

I said a silent prayer that they understood I was still alive. Surely they suspected it would be me purchasing the twenty-thou-sand-dollar comforters our sheep farm sold—the Paris Hilton comforter, we called it. It was a joke product my sisters and I put on the website for our sheep farm, like a lottery ticket. We'd dreamed of Paris Hilton googling herself one day, finding it, and buying one for herself and her dog. She never did, but buying those wildly overpriced quilts for people was really coming in handy as a way to funnel them money. Once upon a time I'd included a note with my purchase of one of the comforters; the note made reference to an inside joke my sisters and I had. It was a way of tipping them off that I was still okay, but that was before I'd faked my death.

I gazed out at the palms and the sea. Everything was wild and beautiful in this life. Intoxicating.

And dangerous.

Odin took one look at me and knew. He always did. "What's wrong?" he asked.

"Nothing," I said.

"Is it the First West job?" he asked, ignoring my lie. "Don't worry about the First West. It's going to be a cakewalk."

"It's a bank, not a tree fort," I said.

"The First West is the loosest bank we've ever seen," Odin said. "We could do it in our sleep even if I didn't hack their security system." We planned to hit it in two days. I would be the driver.

"Yes, I'm nervous for the First West, but it's not that. Maybe I'm just...I don't know."

"Do I have to get it out of you?" Odin's eyes glittered. "I can be persuasive."

"It's just that, things are good. Does that ever spook you? And what were you saying about running out of money?"

"Hey," Zeus said, coming over, tightening his robe belt. "This is a good day. We're here now. Together. With nothing to want for." He slapped the table. "Over here, you guys. Feet. Up."

He put his left foot up on the table, tilted to the side, so you could see his tattoo. Odin and Thor went up next to him and put their feet up, and then I put mine on the very end, making a row of feet—my small and lovely foot and three large man-feet that could definitely use some pedicure action, but we had matching tattoos.

I shivered as I examined my gorgeous tattoo under the protective cellophane wrap. The top of the tattoo was a cloud with big, soulful eyes, brows raised up in fury, lips blowing wind, with four slim, perfectly matched, badass lightning bolts shooting fiercely downward.

We were the four lightning bolts, striking out.

It touched me in a way I could never explain, seeing all our tattooed ankles together. Maybe we were a little bit doomed, but wasn't everybody? And anyway, we were together. Forever.

"It's the most beautiful thing ever," I said.

"*You're* the most beautiful thing ever," Thor said.

"Group hug!" I joked, acting all sarcastic to hide that I wanted to cry.

"I have a better idea. Let's go out and celebrate! We're in LA, baby!" Zeus drained his scotch and threw the glass at the fireplace mantel, where it shattered.

I jumped.

"Jesus, Zeus, that's Waterford crystal." Thor tended to know things like that.

"They'll put it on our bill," he said. "Throw your glasses."

"We are running out of money," Odin said.

"We won't be the day after tomorrow," Zeus said. "In fact, I'm getting bored with these small potatoes banks. I say we knock off something big next month. I say we start thinking about the Prime Royale."

"The Prime Royale First Bank of LA?" Odin barked. "Are you crazy?"

"Then they'll *really* wish we were dead. Actually, that would be a good motto for us." Zeus put up his hands, as if to frame the motto in the air. "You WISH we were dead. Like, you *wish* we were dead but we're not, motherfuckers. Thor, what is that in Latin?"

"*E mords...*something," Thor said.

Zeus frowned. "Better if it's in English." He turned to Odin. "We should add that to the tattoo, on a scroll above the cloud."

"On a banner that angels hold," Odin said.

"Yeah, angels hold it," Zeus said. "You WISH we were dead, motherfuckers. That's what it should say."

"Hold the presses." I put up a hand. "Did you just suggest we add another massively intricate element to that tattoo? Did I just hear you say that?"

"Or maybe it could be a whole new tattoo," Thor said.

Zeus glowered at me. "You enjoyed getting a tattoo, Ice."

"Nobody robs the Prime Royale bank of LA," Odin said.

"That's exactly why we should rob it." Zeus wiped a hand over his mouth. "But first we have to celebrate. I say we hit Guvvey's. She barely met anyone last time. This time we'll officially introduce her to the crème de la crème."

I smiled. *The criminal crème de la crème!*

Chapter Seven

"We'll need nice clothes for Guvvey's," Thor said. "Can we sneak by the hideout and grab our suits?"

Zeus shook his head. "We can't go back there until Manning's done sweeping and monitoring it. Our enemies came too close. We'll hit the hideout after we know it's clean. Only after it's clean. Tonight maybe."

"I'm good with that," I said. "Better safe than sorry."

Odin watched Zeus closely. He had objections.

"What? Our enemies are onto us," Zeus barked at Odin. "We can't wreak vengeance against those who wronged us if we're dead. We let Manning do his job, ensure it's clean."

"I'm not talking about the hideout; I'm talking about the Prime Royale. You seriously want us to knock over the Prime Royale? How is that not a death wish?"

"Because we're awesome at robbing banks," Zeus said. "That's how."

Thor and Odin grumbled.

Our little group was a democracy when it came to hotels and restaurants, but we were an army when it came to criminal activity, and Zeus was the commander in chief.

Why were they feeling so unhappy about the idea of robbing the Prime Royale? What was so different about the it?

"I want to make another safety sweep of the hotel," Thor said. "Let me take Ice to check out the atrium."

Zeus nodded. "Good idea."

I threw on some clothes. My guys had gotten concerned about picking up tails lately. The enemy was getting smarter. We couldn't rest just because I was fake dead.

Five minutes later, Thor and I were strolling off the tenth-floor elevator. This was one of those hotels where rooms looked out over an interior courtyard. You couldn't see that much from this high up...unless you were a super high-functioning criminal who had glasses with a small scope attached to them.

I leaned over the railing next to Thor, who was discreetly examining the people lounging around below. I was giving him cover, making this look like a romantic liaison instead of a spying liaison.

A giant plastic dolphin was suspended from the atrium ceiling, apparently in mid-jump, just hanging there over a reflecting pool far down below.

"Every time I come out here, I just itch to shoot the chain and send that dolphin into that pool down there," Thor said.

I smiled. "And let him complete his jump?"

"I'm not joking. I really want to."

I frowned. "For real? Dude, it's a giant plastic dolphin"

"Yesterday I brought my piece out here. With a silencer."

My heart pounded. "No."

"It's not like it would hit anyone," he said. "It would just fall in the pool."

"There are other problems with shooting down that thing than whether it hits people or not."

"I just wanted to release him. Give him a little resolution." He sounded weary.

"But you know you so shouldn't, right?"

After a bit too much hesitation, he said, "Right. It's just, you know. Mid-jump. He's trapped."

"It's art."

Thor grunted.

The conversation worried me.

I sometimes felt Thor straining at the bonds of this life. Always on the run, taking chances. I thought about a certain experience that might be called the orgasm-while-weaving-around-in-traffic-in-front-of-a-traffic-cop incident, which Thor recklessly incited.

Did he want to get caught? Did he want to bring things to a close?

A life of crime can be hard on people. My guys had been frank about that.

I'd had a difficult time deciding if I should say anything to Zeus about Thor's recklessness that day in the car with the cops and the orgasm. I didn't want to seem like a tattler.

And really, taking dangerous chances with the cops? Did that qualify as a problem in this new world? Flaunting the law was practically in the bank robber job description—right under "ability to effectively communicate hold-up demands" and "outstanding multitasking skills while wearing a mask."

I'd asked Zeus about it in principle a while back—if there were things members should alert each other on.

Like things with Thor? he'd asked me.

Things with anyone, I'd said diplomatically.

Zeus had seen right through me. *I'm well aware of where Thor is at,* he'd said. *I'll figure something out.*

"Imagine seeing it drop into that pool," Thor said, interrupting my train of thought. "Not like anybody would know it was us. They'd think it broke."

"You shouldn't shoot down giant sculptures," I said. "I think that's a rule we could all agree on."

"That's why I want to do it," he whispered. "Because I shouldn't." It was almost a confession.

It was then that I noticed he had his gun out.

"Put that away!" I said.

Thor grinned. "C'mon. It'll be such a spectacle."

"You can't," I said.

"I need to," Thor said.

"You don't need to do that, Thor," I said. "Tell me what you really need."

He just fingered the trigger.

I grabbed his chin and turned his face to me, staring into his blue eyes. "What do you need?" I asked, noting the weariness I saw there. Or was it sorrow?

"Fine." Thor shoved the gun into his pants. "Come on."

We continued on with the second half of the sweep, which involved a spin by the front desk and a stroll through the lower lounge.

Had he really been about to shoot that thing down? Did he want me to stop him? Or did he want me to watch?

I felt so worried. What did he need? He was so smart. Was he not being challenged? Was that the problem?

Zeus and Odin were still lounging in bathrobes when we got back to the hotel room.

"Isis needs a better gown for Guvvey's this time," Thor announced. "She deserves to go out there in style this time."

"Take six large out of the case," Zeus said to Thor. "You and Isis handle it."

"Six is all we have left," Thor said.

"Let's blow it all tonight, then!" Zeus said. "Fuck it!"

"You better not buy me any fashion boy outfits," Odin said.

"We're getting you a double-breasted fancy suit and aviator glasses," I teased.

"That settles it. I'm going with you," Odin said.

"What the hell, we'll all go shopping," Zeus said.

I felt relieved. I wasn't eager to go shopping with Thor alone, what with the reckless mood he seemed to be in.

"We go shopping and out to dinner at Guvvey's," Zeus announced. "It'll be like our first proper date. As a group." He pointed at all of us, one after another, and growled, "It'll be a romantic date with no fucking until afterwards. Got it? Because the four of us are like a couple, and that's final. We are going to have a proper date."

"You are so romantic." I said it like I was joking, but it touched me that Zeus wanted the four of us to have a proper romantic date.

Thor turned to me and said, in his gravelly dirty-talk voice, "Then, after our romantic date, we will use your body mercilessly for our own gratification. We'll tie you up so that you're helpless and then fuck you like a whore."

"Hmm," I said jokingly, as if his words didn't send a jolt of desire into my core.

Odin came over and drew a finger up my neck, stopping at the point below my chin. He tilted up my head, forcing me to stare into his eyes and at the bruise covering his cheekbone. "Is *something-g* amusing?" he asked me.

I swallowed. "No."

He came closer, invading my space. I was feeling wild. I wanted to kiss him on the badass bruise.

"No, I think you are amused, Ice," Odin said. "Do you think we use you like a whore for your *fucking-g* amusement?"

I swallowed, enjoying the feeling of being off-balance by his unpredictability. "No, Odin," I said smoothly. "I don't think you do it for my *gamusement*, no."

Something flared in his eyes. "Oh, Isis." He grabbed my wrists, squeezed. My heart sped. "That is what a naughty goddess says." He walked me backwards until I hit the wall. He pressed me there, panting, looking strangely alive. "Bring me the case with the paddle," he called.

My pulse raced. "The *paddle*?" He'd only ever spanked me with his hand.

"You think this is for your *fucking-g* amusement. It is not."

My heart pounded. Odin always pushed it. He understood me in a way that Zeus and Thor didn't. He understood that thrills and danger called to me.

He lowered his voice. "You will take your punishment, and it will not be easy."

"Jesus," Zeus said. "Are we ever getting out of this hotel room or not?"

"I'll get the case," Thor said.

My insides turned to jelly. Odin nuzzled my cheek with his sandpapery whiskers, and I reveled in it. I felt completely receptive to him, at his mercy.

"You will take it, Isis." He latched on to my earlobe with his teeth, and I melted. My nipples rubbed against the inside of my robe, still incredibly sensitive.

"I didn't technically disobey," I managed to whisper.

He said, "Not technically. But you did, Isis."

"Did we not just agree to a romantic date?" Zeus demanded. He put on his sunglasses and hat, all ready to go, just as Thor came in with a small black case. A case of paddles?

"You're right," Odin said. "We must go on our date first." He pulled away from me, amber eyes glittering, like he'd thought of something dastardly. He took the case from Thor, held it in front of him, unopened. My imagination began to run wild.

"What's in there? D-do you have a lot of paddles?" I asked breathlessly.

"Zeus is right," Odin said. "You will find out what's in the case after our romantic date. And you will feel your punishment as you have felt nothing in your life."

"Hold on," I said. "You won't show me now?" A wild thrill buzzed through me.

"You will wait," he said, watching me watch the case. "And you will contemplate what it means to me that you would make fun of my *fucking-g* accent." He smiled, daring me to say *gaccent*.

I wanted to say it—I wanted to!

Thor took one look at my expression and rolled his eyes. "Sweet Jesus," he said. "Don't say it or we'll never get out of here."

"You want to say it," Odin said. "This, too, I will remember."

I smiled. "You can't get me on what I *want* to do!"

"I can get you on anything," Odin said.

"Not fair!" I protested.

He lowered his voice to a rumble. "I can never be fair where you are concerned, baby."

Heat blossomed between my legs. Whatever dirty punishment Odin had in mind, I wanted it to happen *now*, not tonight.

Odin smiled. He reached out and took the sunglasses Zeus handed him and put them on. They were junky mirrored sunglasses with purple frames in the shape of hearts, like something you'd make your dog wear in Facebook pictures. "Tonight," he said.

With those glasses on, I could no longer see his eyes. Somehow the fact that I couldn't see his eyes increased the thrill factor, which was also amped up by the sheer weirdness of the glasses.

He smiled again. "You like them? Perhaps I will wear them when you receive your punishment. Perhaps I will wear gloves. Perhaps I will be a different person."

"A fashion-challenged sociopath, perhaps?" I teased.

"Perhaps."

I snorted.

He spun around. "Let's go."

It took me a while to collect myself.

I looked over at Thor to find him smirking. He handed me sunglasses and a ball cap and then put on his Greek fisherman's hat and Ray-Bans. Zeus wore a ball cap and aviator glasses.

"We look like we're in disguise," I observed as we left the room. "Like, a little conspicuously in disguise."

"Not in LA," Zeus said. "Incognito blends here."

"People will think we're movie stars," Odin said. "Or more, that we want people to think we're movie stars. Nobody would suspect the truth, that we are among America's most wanted. We love this *fucking-g* place."

Chapter Eight

IT WAS DARK WHEN WE REACHED THE OUTSIDE shopping district. "Do stores stay open all night here or what?" I observed.

"They stay open late, yeah," Thor said. "Bank robbers' hours."

Knocking around as a gang made me feel so good, like we were in on a secret nobody else in the world knew. And all the trouble at home, my grief about my parents dying, missing my sisters, all of that felt far, far away now, especially when I thought about what was coming later...and the mysterious contents of Odin's box.

Thor made us stop at the Croissant Express, the gang's favorite bakery, for almond croissants. We got a bag of them and sat outside the shop at little café tables that situated next to a trellis that was exploding with greenery and flowers and colorful lights. "Celebration food," Thor said, ripping his apart, exposing the creamy almond-stuff center.

"I *fucking-g* missed this place," Odin said, plopping his feet onto a nearby chair and pretty much inhaling his pastry. Much as I loved the exciting high points with my guys, seeing their everyday lives felt precious in a way that was hard to describe. So this was their favorite bakery!

We went to a tuxedo store and got them suited up, though Odin insisted on a tux that was just a little too small, with the dorkiest purple ruffly shirt. He never wanted to look perfect, yet he always did.

Zeus got a sweet black suit with a red shirt underneath.

Thor came out of the dressing room in a suit of white linen and a Panama hat, looking hot and a bit yesteryear.

"What the fuck are you wearing?" Odin growled at him.

"If you got it, flaunt it," Thor said.

I grinned. "You are looking very young writer in 1950s Cuba-ish."

Thor liked that.

They put their normal clothes back on and we went to a dress shop next. I tried on a series of dresses and was dismayed to discover that the eating-and-drinking-with-bank-robbers lifestyle had caused me to put on a few pounds. I finally tried a sexy red number with a fabulously low back that worked with my curves instead of against them.

My criminals were getting all crabby with man-shopping burnout, but they perked up when I strolled out of the dressing room and spun around. "What do you think?"

"Fits like a glove," the salesgirl said.

Odin grinned. "A glove indeed."

"Come here," Thor said.

Zeus just burned at me with his green, green eyes, making me feel super sexy. "We'll take it," he whispered.

"Take it *off*," Odin added.

I felt my face go red, but really, I felt like a queen.

I turned to the pretty blonde salesgirl who seemed a bit stunned by our foursome-ness. "Looks like it's a go," I said proudly. She nodded, expression professionally blank. There was a time where I might have felt weird, but I didn't feel weird now; I just felt lucky.

I sometimes wondered if my guys marveled at us finding each

other the way I marveled at it, like if they sat around when I wasn't there and said, "I can't believe we found a girl who will rob banks with us and let us boss her around and play dirty sex games with her." Because I definitely thought a similar thing about them.

We picked out some shoes. They had to be strappy and not cover my tattoo, which was still settling, according to Odin. I got the feeling they wanted people to be able to see it. I definitely did!

We carried our bags down the moonlit street. It was true—everybody wore sunglasses and hats in this part of town, even in the dark.

We blended in.

I'd heard that LA has a special quality of light like nowhere on earth, and that's one of the reasons the movie studios located there. But there was something sweet and delicious about the moonlight, too.

Thor's blond hair gleamed like polished gold under his dark cap, his skin was fairytale pale, with faint pink on his cheeks, as though he'd spent his life herding reindeer in a tale of yore.

Zeus seemed to occupy more space, somehow, and his green eyes shone.

Odin looked more intense than usual, even with those ridiculous sunglasses. The bruise on his dusky cheekbone had an otherworldly black-and-blue hue.

We stopped at a craft store. I bought a needlepoint kit that had a pattern of a sheep standing in a patch of sunflowers. We continued on past a fancy spa with a sign that advertised romantic couple's massages.

"Wait." Thor stopped in front of the blindingly white polished pillars that marked the entrance. "Let's do a romantic couple's massage," he said. "We're on a romantic date."

"But we're not a couple," I said. "How will we divide up?"

"Fuck that," Thor said. "The four of us are a couple just as much as anybody."

"When they say couple, they mean two," Odin said. "Like hell

I'm getting a couple's massage with Zeus while you get one with Ice."

"I thought we were going to dinner," I said. "At this rate we won't get there until two in the morning."

"Guvvey's does get going late," Odin said.

"We're a romantic unit," Thor argued, unwilling to leave the couple's-massage thing alone. "All of us, right?" He looked at Zeus. Was he trying to goad Zeus? "We're just as much of a couple as anyone."

"Actually, we're not," Odin said.

"Says who?" Thor continued. "Fuck it. We've had our lives pulled out from under us. We've got ZOX on our ass. And now we can't even go for a couple's massage because we're a foursome? Is there not one normal thing left we get to do?"

"Yeah!" Zeus growled, picking up the charge. "We *should* get to do this. The four of us are a fucking couple and that's that. And I want rocks on my back like in the picture, too." With that, Zeus headed in.

"What have you done, Thor?" I breathed.

Thor smiled slyly. Was this what he'd wanted? For Zeus to get riled up? For there to be trouble? Was this just another way of shooting down the dolphin sculpture?

We followed Zeus across the posh, arty lobby which featured lush colors, waterfalls cascading down the walls, and alien-looking glass light fixtures.

"We want a couple's massage," Zeus said when we reached the counter.

The woman at the desk had blue hair with pink accents, and her name tag said Carmella. She looked down at the schedule. "For two couples?"

"No, the four of us are one couple."

She peered up. "Couple's massages are for two."

"But we want one for all of us together," Zeus said. "We'll pay extra. Whatever it takes."

"Rules are rules," she said.

Zeus was looking a bit wild.

Uh-oh.

Thor smiled excitedly. Yes, he'd wanted this, I realized. It seemed more and more clear that Thor wanted trouble. I wondered again if I should say something about the dangerous driving hijinks. And was his idea to shoot down the dolphin a normal thing for a criminal to think about, or something beyond?

Zeus slapped a hundred-dollar bill onto the counter. "Find a way to make it four and charge what you need to charge. Because we, the four of us, are a romantic unit."

Her gaze floated over us and landed on me. Not sure what else to do, I grinned.

"We can't do four, because only two people fit on the large tables," she said.

"Then push two tables together," Zeus growled.

"The practitioners wouldn't be able to reach the center two as well." Carmella shook her head. "They work from the side. I'm sorry."

Odin tensed. If Odin, our most emotionally attuned gang member, was worried, that wasn't good.

"It's okay," I said.

"No, it's not okay," Zeus said.

Odin pulled Zeus away from the counter. "You want them calling the five-oh?" he whispered angrily. "On our romantic date?" I stared at him in his purple glasses. Had he just called the cops the five-oh? El-oh-el!

"No, I want a massage on our romantic date," Zeus said loudly.

"I'm sorry, that's not how we're set up." Carmella went back to her computer.

I bit my lip. Would things get hot? Would guns come out? Zeus seemed so keen on the massage. Then Odin went back to the counter and slapped another hundred-dollar bill on it, and then he leaned over and whispered something to her.

She stared at him, assessing him, it seemed. "Fine. We'll do a foursome massage. One moment, please." She turned and left.

"What did you say to her?" I asked.

"Trade secret," Odin said.

"We don't keep secrets from each other," Zeus said.

Odin smiled. "There needs to be some mystery to keep a relationship alive, honey."

Zeus grabbed Odin's shirt front. "I'll fucking get it out of you, my friend."

"Not here, hopefully," I said in a warning tone. "I've never been in a pretty place like this, and I don't want us to wreck our romantic date." Unlike Thor, I was not up for additional mayhem.

Zeus released Odin. "Fine," he bit out.

We ended up in a room with two large tables pushed together, and all of us lying side by side. Four bodyworkers rubbed our feet and backs while we drank champagne and talked about nothing.

I was between Zeus and Thor, and Odin was on the far side of Thor. Odin was in the doghouse, I guess, for not telling Zeus what he whispered. Still, he was getting a better massage because he was on the end.

It was actually very romantic, and it was kind of like a date.

Later, the workers came and put smooth, warm rocks on our backs like Zeus demanded. The weight and the heat of the rocks felt sensual and relaxing.

Odin was the first to say it. "These rocks on my back make me want to fuck."

"Me too," Thor said.

"This a romantic date for Isis," Zeus said. "We don't fuck until we get back to the hotel. Or home, if it's ready."

Odin said, "I seem to recall her agreeing to our rules, and our rules are we fuck her when we want."

"We said this was a romantic date," Zeus said. "Don't you

think Isis deserves some romance?" He turned his head to me. "That's what you want, right?"

I smiled. I sort of wanted to fuck, actually, but not here. "We've trashed on these people and this place enough," I said. "I don't think they want us fucking in here."

The weight of his eyes on me felt more intense and more erotic than the weight of the stones.

"But what do *you* want?" Odin asked from the other side of Thor.

"To have this nice date like we are having right now," I said. "Doing anything with you guys is nice. Just lying here. It's nice."

Odin groaned.

Just then, a man came back with a golden platter full of new rocks. He replaced our old ones and refilled our champagne glasses.

Zeus was the first to get bored. He took the rocks off his own back and left the room for lord knows where.

Odin came and stretched out on my other side. Like old times, me and Thor and Odin.

"And then we can take you home after," Thor said. "Just like a real date. We'll be old-fashioned."

"I'll be going for Medieval," Odin said. "But that's still old-fashioned, right?"

My insides warmed.

"There is a room in our hideout that has certain Medieval elements," Thor said.

"Like what?" I imagined something dungeon-y.

Odin slid a hand under the sheet, making contact with my ass. "Some mystery is good to keep in a relationship, but we will bring our box of paddles. Or use the ones there. Very wicked ones. And maybe chains."

The anticipation was killing me.

Later, we all took a steam bath together without having sex, which was hard with my guys all sweaty and naked. I wanted to have sex, but Zeus was fixated on this romantic date thing. Like he wanted to make it perfect for me.

On the way back to our black SUV, Zeus suddenly got it in his head to stop and buy four wildly expensive, weirdly flavored waters from a sidewalk vendor. We all followed him to the little booth, where he took his time to choose one for each of us.

My guys got really quiet and deliberate, like it was the most important decision on the planet.

What was up? Usually they didn't care about things like waters.

Odin furrowed his brow after Zeus paid. "Where?" Odin asked.

"Three o-clock," Zeus said. "Follow me and look in this store. Eyes forward."

Uh-oh.

Something was definitely up.

I followed my guys' lead. After we got waters, we all stopped in front of a cell phone store to look in the window at the gadgets. Did they want new cell phones now? But then I realized I was the only one looking in the window at the gadgets. My guys, ever the bandits, were looking at the reflection of the street behind us.

"We picked him up at the massage place," Zeus added.

"What's going on?" I asked.

"A tail," Thor said.

"Cops," Odin said. "And there are two of them."

"Let's hope it's just cops," Thor said darkly.

Chapter Nine

We headed into a random nightclub. Zeus pulled off his hat and sunglasses and handed the hostess a few hundreds, winking at her. "We're looking for a friend," he said, like it was secret between them.

She smiled and pocketed the bills. "Go on in, then."

As we crossed the dark interior, Thor took off his hat and glasses. So did Odin. I followed suit. Apparently it was *disguises off* time.

Deep in the dark club, Zeus handed a busboy more hundreds. "We want to say *hi* to a friend." Without waiting for an answer, he pushed through the kitchen door.

Thor grabbed my hand and pulled. "Just follow."

There were protests in the kitchen until Zeus slapped a pile of hundreds on the stainless-steel counter. The man was a regular Robin Hood tonight. "For your awesome work tonight, guys. Keep it up." Then he turned and led us out the back. We burst out into the cool night air and walked fast down an alley and across another street.

Finally, we slowed.

"Did we lose them?" I asked.

"Yup," Thor said.

"They were just plainclothes," Odin said. "They weren't going to do anything."

Zeus said, "I didn't like his shoes. They didn't say cop to me."

"He was a cop," Odin said.

"What did you say at the massage place?" Zeus demanded.

"What does it matter?" Odin said. "You were about to pull out your piece and go hot."

Zeus just grumbled in response.

"What if it's ZOX?" I asked. "And that dangerous, horrible Agent Denko?"

Zeus slung an arm around me. "If it's ZOX, then it's ZOX. Is anybody following us now?"

"I guess not," I said.

"Are we safe right now? And together? Are we fucking awesome right now?" he asked.

"I guess," I said.

"The answer is yes," Zeus said. "Yes, we're all of the above."

Guvvey's was livelier this time around, maybe because it had been relatively early when we'd met with Tabby, whereas now the club was in full swing.

But it was even more than that. When we'd come before, I was just a friend of the gang. Now I was an official member, with a tattoo to prove it. I felt like a debutante at a ball—the newest member of the God Pack. My heart pounded a little bit faster just thinking about it. Whatever my guys were into, that's what I wanted to be into. They were my allies now, and I was theirs.

I wanted to help them.

I wanted to save them.

I didn't know what that meant, really, but there had to be a way to save them. Because seriously, how long could they go on living this dangerous lifestyle?

Drinks were served. Lots more people came around, and I showed my tattoo some more. Thor ordered us the appetizer flight and the dinner flight.

"You've got the menu memorized?" I asked.

"You get whatever they're serving here. Like when you go to somebody's house," he explained.

"What if I don't like it?" I asked.

Odin narrowed his eyes. "You have to eat it. Even if you don't like it. Or *else.*"

Thor hit Odin on the arm. "Stop teasing her. You don't have to eat it, Isis."

A cheer went up from the dance floor where a tough-looking man in a tux with a machine gun slung over his back was doing a robot dance.

The guy looked so strong and dangerous, even in the tux. The dyed yellow ends of his hair shone like a bright, badass crown over his dark roots. Yet he was dancing like a freak.

"That's something you don't see every day," I said.

"That's Matteo," Zeus observed grimly. "There was exactly one other crew who would ever consider taking down the Prime Royale bank, and that's Matteo's old crew, but the rest of them are locked up now. The Prime Royale is all ours."

"Would you get off the Prime Royale?" Odin snapped, downing his scotch. "They didn't take it down because it's stupid to try."

"I thought Matteo joined the Giraffes after his crew got arrested," Thor said.

"The Giraffes booted him out," Zeus said. "He's back to having no gang."

"Hold on, the Giraffes?" I asked. "There's a bank takeover robbery gang called the Giraffes?"

"They don't do takeovers," Zeus said. "They're all about jewels."

Odin sniffed. "*Fucking-g* Giraffes."

"Seriously? The Giraffes?" I repeated. "Who would name their criminal gang after an animal whose only natural advantage is the ability to eat leaves off treetops?" It seemed weird in light of the murals. And just...weird, period.

"Most people call them the Gigis," Thor said, which didn't exactly clear up the mystery.

The waiter delivered our appetizers. Tapenade, bruschetta, fancy cheeses, crab puffs. A breadbasket and mini bottle of olive oil with a spout, just like a normal Italian restaurant. Somehow, I'd expected less regular food. Maybe weirdly giant, King-Henry sized drumsticks or octopus tentacle soup or something.

"Do the Giraffes threaten to munch on people's potted palms if they don't give them all of their jewels?"

"Don't underestimate the Giraffes," Odin said. "They've got a streak of chaos a mile wide."

"The God Pack is a way better name than the Giraffes," I said, grabbing a piece of bread.

My guys agreed.

We feasted and drank and talked.

When the appetizers were gone, I leaned against Zeus and let Odin inspect the healing of my tattoo. Odin kept my feet in his lap when his inspection was finished, and Zeus kept an arm flung around me. Thor lounged at the very end, his lanky self stretched out elegantly.

"I heard once that Matteo had intel on the Prime Royale," Zeus said.

"Then why didn't he and his old crew hit it?" Odin asked.

"Good question," Zeus said. "If they had intel on the Prime, they would've hit it."

"No, they wouldn't, because they'd know it was fucked up to try," Odin said. "That's my point here."

"They're also not as good at robbing banks as we are," Thor said. "Let's recall, they *did* do mostly supermarket bank jobs."

Zeus twisted his big, beautiful, thuggish man lips into a sneer. "Supermarket banks." Apparently, supermarket banks were way beneath my bandits. "Anyway, I want to know if Matteo has intel on the Prime."

I ate a roll while my bandits discussed Matteo's sources and the possibility of his having good intel.

Odin waved to a stout guy in a tuxedo. He guy sauntered over, smoking a cigar. "And then they were four," he said.

Thor grinned and introduced us to Bentley. Bentley complimented the tattoo, and it came to me, from the way he talked about it, that everyone in the place had noticed the tattoo.

It made me feel proud.

"Bentley, is it true Matteo's got a line on the Prime?" Zeus asked.

Bentley sat down next to Thor. "That man's got a whole file on the Prime Royale from what I hear."

"No shit," Zeus said. "Why not rob it?"

"Aside from the fact that nobody robs the Prime Royale?" Bentley joked.

"Why get the file, then?"

"To impress the G's," Bentley said. The G's, I took it, were the Giraffes, aka the Gigis. "Those girls are interested in the Prime."

Thor narrowed his eyes. "The Giraffes are jewel thieves, not bank robbers."

"Exactly," Bentley said. "Not their skill set. But the Liz Taylor jewels are in there. A lot of jewels they want are in the Prime Royale."

"Giraffes love their jewels, that's for sure," Odin said.

"Not when those jewels are locked in a bank." Bentley puffed on his cigar. "They don't love that. Banks are not their jam."

They gossiped about Matteo and some other crime figures.

Apparently, the crème de la crème of the LA criminal underground gossiped as much as high school kids.

Bentley left, and Zeus and Odin argued some more about hitting the Prime Royale. Some time later, another man came up, a bespectacled blond man in a brocade jacket. He seemed unhappy, or maybe he was just really serious.

The brocade jacket guy sighed and gave Zeus a key ring, a small notebook and a cell phone, and said he'd bring some gadget later. They talked about eyes on the neighborhood and the terrain being clean. The conversation was sort of technical, and I zoned out. It was late, maybe three in the morning.

My legs were still resting over Odin's lap, and he trailed his fingers up my shin, underneath the cover of the tablecloth, as they all talked.

"That was Manning," Odin said once the man was gone.

I squinted. *Manning*. They'd said the name earlier. "He seems a bit odd."

"He is a bit odd, but odd people are often great at their jobs. He's the AV guy who was at our place," Odin said. "He checked it out and put in new surveillance around the perimeter and the surrounding neighborhood. We get to go back now. You know what that means, Isis?" His fingers trailed up past my knee, now, inching up my inner thigh. "Can you guess?"

My belly tightened. Yes, I could guess what it meant. I could have a lot of fun guessing, in fact. We'd go back to their place, where they apparently had lots of exotic sexual implements and a case of paddles and even a Medieval sex room of some sort.

Odin gave me a heated look as he inched his fingers up a bit more, pushing my dress along with it, his strong hand stark against my pale, freckled skin.

I felt Zeus's hot breath on my ear, and I closed my eyes.

My insides trembled as Odin touched me even higher, his movement concealed by the table and the darkness of our corner. It was super hot, here in the middle of the crowd. "You know what it means?" Odin asked again. He loved making me answer rhetorical questions.

My core pulsed. "I know what it means," I said.

"Say what it means," Zeus said from behind me.

I swallowed as his hands roamed possessively over my stomach.

"Say it," he commanded.

I opened my eyes and glanced over at the wall mural with the antelope getting its neck bitten. Things were feeling wild suddenly.

Dangerous.

I liked it.

I imagined the outlaws in the place knew how my guys were touching me, even though they couldn't see. And I really wanted Odin to keep moving his hand, to reach between my legs, to touch me there. I tightened my pelvic muscles as if that would somehow draw him. I wanted to get off in front of all these people and for them not to know.

"Say what it means," Zeus pursued.

I grinned. This teasing business worked as a two-way street.

Thor's gaze from across the table felt heavy on my skin. "Maybe we should go now."

"No, this is a proper date with dinner on the way," Zeus said. "We're not leaving early just because we want to fuck. But Isis can demonstrate a full understanding of what will happen when we get home."

Heat arrowed through me.

Thor smiled.

"The paddle," I said. "That's what it means."

"The paddle what?" Thor asked, swirling his scotch, always wanting to maximize the dirty talk.

"Odin'll whack me with it," I said.

Thor rolled his eyes. Apparently, *whack* was not a dirty enough word. "Isis, we will bring you home and strip off your dress and your panties so that you're naked in front of us."

"We'll rip it right down the middle," Zeus said.

"Not this dress," I protested.

"Everything is ours," Thor continued, "to do with as we please. You. The dress. Do you remember our deal?"

I closed my eyes, clenching my sex in an exciting way. "Umm..."

"Do you remember?" Odin asked. "Answer."

"Yes, fine," I said. "I obey every order."

"You'll be bare to us," Thor said. "And don't think Odin has forgotten how you made fun of his accent today. Open your eyes, Isis."

I opened my eyes, pulse racing. Thor swirled his drink some more.

"Then we will take you down to a certain room, and we'll tie you up on something..." He glanced over at Odin. "Smooth and leathery."

Odin nodded and inched his fingers up farther, rough fingers on my smooth flesh, inching up the hem to expose my thighs and then my panties behind the cover of the table.

The contrast of the cool air on my skin and Zeus's warmth behind me was getting more intense, heightened by the champagne and the public nature of this whole encounter.

Long story short: I was getting way too aroused for my pants!

Thor continued, looking dashingly evil. "We'll lay you out and help ourselves to you, touching you in ways you can't begin to imagine. How many hands is that?"

"I'm not that drunk," I said, concentrating on Odin's hand caressing my thigh, brushing ever so lightly between my legs, like a feather stroke on the outside of my thong.

"How many, Isis?" Thor asked, like it was the dirtiest question ever.

Odin slid his fingers down and then back up to graze my damp panties again. Lightly, too lightly, stoking my heat.

I closed my eyes. "Six."

"Maybe, Isis," Thor said. "We'll see. The point is that you will be spread out before us. At our mercy. Tied up for our total and complete pleasure. There are so many things I want to do to you." He trailed off, then. "God, where's our food?"

My legs trembled helplessly under Odin's touch. "Maybe we should get it to go," I said.

"The fuck we will," Zeus growled. "This is a proper date."

I smiled. It was anything but proper.

Thor raised one eyebrow. "Six hands is how many fingers, Isis?"

I swallowed with difficulty. "Sixty. I mean thirty."

Zeus chuckled behind me. He moved his hand lower, down to my mound, but not to my clit, where I desperately wanted it. I pressed up my pelvis, but he pushed me back down, firmly. I could feel the excitement radiating off of him, could feel his massive cock pulsing with need. Thor's little narrative was getting to him, too.

I moved my hand behind me into his lap, wrapping my fingers slowly around the bulge that his cock made through his pants.

He sucked in a breath. "This isn't going the way of a proper date," he grated out. But he didn't move my hand.

I wished we were anywhere else. Ideally, at their hideout. I just wanted to have sex with my bandits. I wanted us all to fuck. And then there was the promise of the paddle...I'd enjoyed being spanked, it was true, but a hand is soft. A paddle isn't. The danger made it thrilling. The element of the unknown.

I looked over at the crowd. Nobody would ever guess about the outrageous heat level at our table. Most everyone watched Matteo dance on and on like a robot. He was actually really good at it.

"Look at me," Thor said.

I looked over. There was more?

Zeus shifted behind me, and my nipples grazed against the fabric of my dress.

Thor sipped his scotch, fixing me with his eyes, continuing in his gravelly and hypnotic way. "Once you're all tied up and helpless, begging us to let you come, Odin will bring out that box. I know you've thought about it, Isis."

Shivers went over me.

"Have you been thinking about it?" Thor asked.

"A little," I confessed.

Thor smiled devilishly. "And you will be tied up on your belly, and your ass will be bare to Odin in the cool air. To all of us. And you will wait like that for Odin to bring out the paddle. You will be so wound up, you will crave anything we give you at that point. You will be grateful for any sensation. But do you know what? He won't use the paddle right away."

Zeus shifted again. "Maybe we should stop this talk."

Thor crossed his legs and continued. "Instead, Odin will bring the box around to where you can see it. He'll hold it in front of you, so that you can inspect it and know what it looks like. Do you know why?"

"No," I breathed as Odin crept his hand closer to my throbbing clit. It was driving me wild that he would only touch me there lightly. I wanted some pressure, ideally in the form of a stroke, but my guys could get contrarian when I made requests like that, so I stayed cool.

Thor continued. "When you know what it looks like, you will be able to picture it and feel it when he brings it down on your bare ass. In punishment for your insolence today."

"Wait. I have an addition," Zeus panted. "She inspects the paddle while she sucks me off."

"Okay, good," Thor said, nodding.

I didn't see how this would work exactly, how I would be able to inspect the paddle while Zeus's cock was in my mouth...unless I was sideways maybe, but who needs realistic sex choreography for a hot scenario? I was going with it.

"Isis, Zeus will press his rock-hard cock all the way into your warm, wet mouth. You'll close your lips around him and blow him properly while you examine your tool of erotic punishment."

"Okay," I said, like it made sense.

I felt Zeus's breath speed up even more. Odin inched in closer to me. I grabbed his hand and pushed it between my legs—I couldn't help it! The pressure felt glorious.

Odin pulled away his hand and grabbed my wrist. "Is that proper for a date?" he growled. "To fondle yourself? To force me to?"

"I think it's proper for *this* date," I said.

"Oh dear." Odin shook his head sternly, keeping hold of my hand.

"Can I stop being interrupted?" Thor said.

I heaved out a breath. There was more? Could somebody get off on dirty talk alone? It seemed like that was where things were headed.

"While you inspect the paddle and take Zeus's cock *fully* into your mouth, I am going to pour oil onto your virgin asshole, and then I'll press something cool and firm into it. Larger than fingers. It's time."

I hissed out a breath. It sounded so dirty and exciting. I wanted to do everything, suddenly. Now!

"Hold on," Zeus said. "What?"

Thor said, "She's ready."

"No," Zeus said. "Virgin asshole? Isis, you've never been buttfucked?"

"No," I said.

I felt this tremor go through Zeus, like he'd swallowed hard. "And you'd wish to?" he grated out.

"Oh, yes," I whispered.

"Right now?" he asked.

I frowned, like I was so confused. "But I thought this was a proper date. I don't know what etiquette guides say, but I'm guessing that a proper date doesn't involve a woman getting a hard cock pressed into her virgin asshole in a restaurant." I wished I'd said that dirtier. I wanted to be good at dirty talking too! "Or something else, like maybe smooth and slick. Slowly in."

Thor grinned.

"Especially if maybe another man is fondling her breasts," I added.

Uh! *Fondling.* Who says fondling?

But Zeus swallowed.

"And touching elsewhere as well," I added.

"Where else? Tell him where else," Thor said.

"My, uh, cunt," I said. It wasn't convincing at all, but apparently it worked.

"Fuck it!" Zeus slid out of the booth and stood. He strolled over and said something to our waiter, gesturing at the table.

Odin snickered softly and let go of my hand.

Zeus grabbed the olive oil container. "Follow me."

"What?" I said.

"Follow. Now," Zeus said.

I slid out and stood, smoothing my dress, heart racing.

Thor smiled at me. Such a troublemaker. Had he woven that whole story just to take advantage of Zeus's difficulty with impulse control? Was he playing the mischievous puppeteer yet again?

Odin pressed a warm hand to my bare back. "Wish granted."

"Here?"

"Goddess," Odin said. "Do you need me to answer that?"

WE FOLLOWED ZEUS ACROSS THE PLACE, PAST MORE OF their bizarre criminal comrades, and through an unmarked door that opened onto a small stairwell.

The butterflies in my belly fluttered like mad as we took the stairs down, single file—Zeus, then me, then Thor and Odin. None of us spoke, which made it more dramatic and exciting in a wildly dirty way.

We arrived in a massive storeroom full of metal wire shelving—three aisles of it—stretching on and on into the darkness. The shelving held large bags and jars and cases of wine and booze, and the place smelled faintly of oregano. A storage room for Guvvey's?

"What are we doing here?" I asked.

Zeus took a few steps down an aisle and stopped in front of some empty shelving. He pulled out the actual shelf so that it was just a shelving frame, like a metal square. He turned to me. "How does that look?"

"Is that a rhetorical question?" I asked.

Zeus lowered his voice to a rumble. "Come here."

My belly tightened.

Thor clinked the ice in his drink. "After you, Isis."

I went, heels clicking, right up to Zeus, who waited by the thing, which looked like a place to hang clothes or something. Thor followed me.

Zeus handed the oil to Thor and began to remove his tie, watching me levelly. "It'll do." His gaze had me vibrating.

I felt Odin come up behind me and slowly unzip my zipper.

"Oh," I said, as the dress fell off, pooling around my shoes. I waited, heart racing, wearing nothing but a thong and high heels, standing like an offering before my three gods.

I felt like we were hidden in the deepest corner of the universe together. A place where anything could happen. Would we butt-fuck now? Is that what was going to happen?

Zeus wrapped a beefy hand over the bar at the top of the rack. "Come here, Isis."

Heat flared between my legs. I walked to him on trembling legs.

"Stand here. Can you reach this?" he asked.

I found I could if I kicked off my shoes and stood on the bar below. Butterflies rampaged around in my belly. I loved not knowing what was going to happen.

Before I'd joined my guys, I'd sneak off the sheep farm to do rural extreme sports, which usually involved jumping off some-where I shouldn't be jumping off of, giving myself to the thrill of gravity, the rush of no-turning-back. Now I gave myself to my kinky bank robbers.

"Both hands." His breath sounded ragged.

I grabbed the cool upper bar with both hands.

Zeus whooshed out a breath and came up flush to me, pressing himself to my near-naked flesh, a rough caress of scratchy wool against tender skin. "We are going to make this good for you. You trust us, right?"

"With everything," I said, vibrating with excitement.

He looped his tie over the bar at the top and wrapped it around my wrists, just tightly enough to keep my hands in place.

His shirt grazed my nose as he worked, and I breathed him in. Just the scent of him was lulling me into a strange erotic trance.

When he was done, he stepped away and gazed into my eyes as I hung there, arms overhead, helpless before him, a virgin sacrifice.

A butt-virgin sacrifice, anyway.

Slowly, he slid his hands up and down my arms, watching my eyes. Then he pressed against me so that I could feel the bulge of his cock on my belly. "I know this isn't a proper date," he said, panting, breath hot on my nose.

"I don't want it proper."

He kissed me. "Don't lie. I know it's not. It's just that Thor's talk put the idea in my head. And then you said you wanted it in the ass, with us touching you...Isis, you're such a pathetic dirty talker, I don't know why it got me so wild, but it did. Your pathetic dirty talk is so sexy, I couldn't get it out of my mind." Zeus pressed against me, pushing against me, closing his mouth over my earlobe.

I exhaled sharply, gripping the cool bar above. This was already the best thing ever.

Ice clinked in the darkness.

Thor.

I shot a glance over at him and he smiled. He'd started it; he was to blame. Or, more, to thank. I couldn't think of any place I'd rather be.

Odin just stood there looking hot and devilish in spite of his purple sunglasses.

"Oh, Isis." Zeus kissed my lips, kissed my neck, then closed his mouth over my nipple, sucking it to a pert tip.

Electricity crackled through me, heading straight down between my legs.

Confident hands slid down my hips. Up, then down.

I gripped the hard, cool metal, consumed by the magic of his touch, by the sound of skin against skin, by the sound of his breathing in hushed storeroom.

Wicked fingers looped through my thong and pushed it down my legs.

Odin.

"Are you ready for this?"

"Yes," I said. "Please."

"You're sure?"

My skin sprung alive with pleasure everywhere he touched. "More than sure."

Zeus pulled away. "Gimme that oil, Thor."

Thor handed it to him, and he walked around to the back of the rack. I couldn't see him, but I could feel the brush of his dinner jacket.

Thor looked over at Odin and gestured toward me.

Odin threw off his jacket and his glasses. He came to me and kissed me, looking more beautiful than ever, and open, too, like a flower, though I know he'd hate the comparison.

"Odin," I breathed.

"I didn't want to wait either, goddess." He kissed my breast. I wanted to touch him, to shove my hands into his gorgeous hair, but it wasn't for now, considering my hands were tied above me.

I felt him unbutton his fly, felt the metal of his belt brush my knees as his pants fell. A condom wrapper crinkled.

Zeus's hands roamed possessively over my butt cheeks, sliding along. He'd dipped into the oil—I could tell from the slickness of his fingertips.

My clit tingled as he slipped a slick finger between my butt cheeks and slid it up and down along my hole, teasing me.

I'd never look at olive oil dispensers on restaurant tables the same way ever again.

Just in time, Odin pressed his hips into mine from the front, allowing his cock to stroke along my seam. My brain melted at the devilishly slippery stroking; Odin in front, Zeus in back. We got up a slow, grinding rhythm, erotic and pulsing.

There was the sound of hard breathing, and I realized it was me, that I was panting to the rhythm, harder and harder.

Thor roamed over to where I could see him, and he eyed me knowingly. He was up to something.

"This might be even better than knocking over the Prime Royale," Zeus said.

Odin pressed his fingers against my heated core, slid two fingers along my wet folds.

I gasped softly at his touch.

"You are so wet for us," Odin said. "You want it."

"Yes, yes," I whispered, closing my eyes, reveling in the sensation of his fingers stroking me, pushing me nearer and nearer to the edge.

"Eyes open, Isis," Thor said, voice hot and hypnotic.

I obeyed, and found his cool, blue gaze.

So that was it, then. He planned to be the director, and to keep me excruciatingly aware that he was standing there in his fine suit while I hung helplessly like a naked piece of meat.

He wanted me to know that he'd be watching me get ravished by two men.

His watching doubled the excitement.

"Look at you," Thor whispered as if on cue, as if he was reading my mind.

My breath sped.

"Look at Zeus and Odin using your body for their pleasure," he added.

"Oh, yes," I said stupidly, but what do you say to that? "Yes."

Zeus pushed his finger harder along the seam, nearly penetrating my asshole. "You like this?"

"Yes," I said, feeling faint.

Zeus growled. "You are such a fucking thrill whore."

I gasped as he pressed his finger just a little bit in, but then he pulled it back out, curling wickedly up and down along the seam.

Thrill whore. Takes one to know one, I thought. We were all thrill whores.

He pushed his finger in deeper this time, ending this train of thought. Ending all thought, for that matter. At least all thought that was happening inside my head.

"You get off on the thrill of being fucked by two bank robbers while one watches," Zeus growled.

"Yes, I do," I said helplessly.

Odin bit my earlobe.

"Ode," I breathed.

"Isis, wrap your legs around Odin," Thor said. "Help her, Odin.

"Wait," Odin grated. Roughly, he grabbed my knee and pulled up my leg. I felt the head of his cock pressing to my sex, felt him guide it in.

I gasped as he pushed into me, filling me exquisitely. He reached around and grabbed my butt cheeks, lifting most of my weight off my arms as I swung my other leg around him.

He began to fuck me slowly, supporting me.

I closed my eyes, unsure if I could last. Did I need to think about sheep breeds again?

"Stay with us," Thor said.

I opened my eyes, fixing my gaze on Thor. That's when I felt Zeus press two fingers into my asshole, slick and slippery with oil. He had better access now that my legs were wrapped around Odin.

"You are so tight," Zeus breathed, finger fucking my asshole, in and out. "You want me to fuck you here?" Zeus asked.

"Yes," I whispered, voice sounding drugged. "I definitely do."

Odin stilled, pulled out. And then I felt it, Zeus's cock against my asshole.

"Breathe, goddess," Thor said, crossing his legs, leaning back on a box, watching. "Odin, pull her ass cheeks wide for Zeus."

I waited for Odin to comply. I felt his magical fingers dig into my ass cheeks, pulling me wider as his own cock pressed against my slit, teasing me.

Strangely, Odin's holding my ass cheeks wide only made Zeus's cock feel bigger at my oil-slickened asshole. His head felt round, like a ball probing at my asshole.

Then he gripped my hips and pushed in, slowly.

His cock in my ass was a blunt surprise at first—it felt like a bowling pin pushing inside me!

But then I relaxed, felt my body take him, and it was just right. More than right—it turned into a delicious fullness. He pressed in deep, and when I thought he was all the way in, he filled me more.

"Oh, wow." Total bliss washed through me, like he'd hit some dark trigger that flooded me with pleasure hormones. Relentlessly he pressed into me. It was so intense and dirty to have his cock pushed into my ass, I thought my entire brain might unravel.

Odin's fingers tightened on the flesh of my butt cheeks, and he pressed his cock back into me.

They both filled me.

And then they began to thrust.

They started slowly at first, going at different paces: Zeus's movements were heavy and ponderous. Odin fucked me at a slightly faster pace.

Or was it the other way around?

I tried to figure out specifically what was happening, like I somehow needed to keep track of it all, but it was difficult, thanks to the keen pleasure building up in the pit of my pelvis. But then I realized I didn't need to track whose cock was whose. It's not as if I was going to get a quiz later...though you never could say what my bandits would come up with next. Maybe there would be a quiz.

It was a quiz that I would gladly fail. My pleasure kept getting stoked higher by the constant and mind-blowing invasion of two cocks in me. I almost needed them to stop, because the pleasure was building too big, too fast. I felt as if my body was no longer mine, like I was being fucked into a chaos of pleasure.

Was the intensity too much? I was spinning, the inside of my brain glittering with pleasure.

"Breathe," Thor said again. "Just give in. You have no choice."

I breathed. I gave myself over to the two cocks inside me. To the two bodies against me. An out-of-control spiral in my belly.

I groaned with pleasure as they filled me. The feeling changed; it was like I'd left firm ground for some kind of fairy wind. I was nothing but feeling as they thrust in and out.

Thor's voice. Something about fucking me in unison. Again, he wanted me to look at him.

I managed somehow to open my eyes and look at Thor.

He leaned back with his scotch, swirling it smugly in the half shadows, holding my gaze. "You look amazing," he whispered. "Like a dirty goddess. Just look at you."

Then, without warning, Odin took my nipple into his mouth and bit. I gasped. Right then, it was all over.

I cried out as my muscles clenched and clutched madly against the fullness of two cocks buried inside me.

Zeus and Odin's movements got jerky and rough.

One in, one out. Both in, both out, what did I care?

"Omigod," I breathed.

Zeus kissed the back of my neck—sloppily, frantically.

Odin threw back his head and rammed into me hard. He stayed deep inside, groaning. I felt the frantic pulse of his cock as he came.

"Yes, Odin," I said.

"*Uh, uh, uh,*" Zeus said. His hands gripped my hips and squeezed as he pushed into me one last time, moaning.

I don't know how long the three of us stayed entangled. I felt us come down together, first mentally, then physically.

I unlocked my legs from Odin's waist and stood on my own two feet on the bar below. I felt Zeus's shaky fingers untying my hands. I swayed against him.

"Whoa." Odin caught us both from falling.

"Fuck." Zeus sunk down onto the floor and pulled me onto his lap.

Thor walked up with a handful of white towels. "Here ya go, party people." He threw them at us.

Zeus wiped the warm, wet cloth between my legs. "Fuck, Isis. It wasn't your romantic date, but..."

Odin snorted, cleaning himself up. "That was more *fucking-g* romantic than eating Guvvey's bistro food."

"I love this date," I said. "This date is going really well."

Zeus stood me up and smoothed my hair. "Lemme get your dress."

Odin put his mirrored purple sunglasses back on and circled his arms around my waist. "Don't think this gets you out of anything later."

I pushed my hands through his hair, like I'd wanted to all along. "I don't think it."

"You are so beautiful," Odin said.

I stopped myself from saying it back. Instead, I said, "And you are a wicked motherfucker."

He paused, watching my eyes, then he kissed me fiercely, with an abandon that was uncharacteristic for him.

We made our way back up and out into the nightclub.

Waiters brought our dinner as soon as we sat back down at our table. Maybe they were holding it for us.

The place got more and more crowded as we ate. It had to be four in the morning, I figured. I said something about the time and Thor pointed out that this was the end of the workday for a lot of these people.

I hadn't thought of that, but it made sense.

"I'm going to the ladies' room," I said, throwing my napkin onto the table.

Thor pointed at a pink glow on the other side of the bar. "Door's over on the other side. Like an escort, goddess?"

"I think I can make it." I grabbed my silver clutch and headed across the place, past the dance floor, which was empty now. Matteo had wearied of his robot dancing, it seemed.

I headed around the bar, still a little shaky from the sex—it was so intense, in a good way. I loved the thrill of being beholden to my guys. It was like extreme sports, but sexier.

I pushed through the pink door into a spa-like bathroom with lots of plants, and a lounge area that opened into a mirrored wall. After I peed, I put on pink lipstick. Now that I'd changed my long red hair to short platinum hair, pink makeup worked for me.

I snapped my clutch shut, ruffled my hair just so, and washed my hands, then turned to see three very striking women who hadn't been there before, lounging in the seating area all cool, just staring at me, looking very roguish.

"Hey," I said.

One of them stood. She was about a foot taller than me, dressed in white leather pants and a white silk blouse that contrasted with the shiny black gun in her holster and the deep brown of her skin. Her hair was dyed as bright as mine, but shorter, in rough little curls.

"You're the sheep farmer," she said.

Chapter Eleven

"Ex-sheep farmer," I clarified.

"I'm Macy Gigi," the woman said, holding out a hand in the lounge-like bathroom. "But you can call me Macy."

"The Giraffes," I said, taking her hand. It made sense. They were so leggy, what with those shoes and outfits.

"Yup," Macy said.

"Cool," I said, sort of stupidly.

She introduced me to Angel Gigi, who had brown eyes and lots of tattoos and wore a red chiffon party dress that looked very 1950s; her long hair was dyed a light caramel, and she had a tiara. Jenny Gigi had a golden suntan and white-blonde hair. She looked like a stripper.

Macy came right up to me. "We have a lot of names because that's what we like. We switch out names as often as we switch out hair colors."

I nodded and smiled as we shook hands. It didn't strike me as the most efficient naming system ever, but who was I to judge?

"Nice tattoo," Jenny said from behind me.

"Let's see." Macy patted the counter. "Come on, I just want to see," she added when I hesitated.

These Gigis were so...outlandish. And they wore outrageously high-heeled platform shoes. I put up my foot and let them check out my gang tattoo. Showing it off made me feel incredibly proud. The tattoo told the world that if anybody messed with me, they messed with the God Pack.

"Odin does some nice work," Macy said. "So you all have four lightning bolts now?"

"Yeah. I got the whole thing, and they all got an extra bolt." I tried to act like it was no big, and not an entire afternoon of me saying *eep* and acting like a baby.

"Sweet. But the shoes are a little sad," Angel said. "Your boys pick those out for you?"

"We picked them out together."

"Yeah, right. Means your guys picked 'em out. Guys have shit taste in shoes." Macy fixed me with a gaze; her silver eyeliner and silver fake lashes made her brown eyes appear strangely deep and dark. "You get tired of taking orders from little boys..." She whipped a card out of her pocket and held it toward me with elegant fingers. The card was smaller and thicker than a normal business card, with rounded corners. "We know you drive, Isis. And we hear you've got nerve. We're down a member due to some grievous disrespect on the part of our last member. You don't seem the disrespecting type." She smiled. "You get tired of those dudes, you call us."

"I won't get tired of those dudes," I said coolly. "Ever. We're together."

Macy smiled. "Gotcha." She pushed the card closer to me. "Still, no reason you can't make new friends, right?"

It was weird. As soon as she said it, I realized something I was deeply missing: female companionship, aka girlfriends! I'd spent my life surrounded by sisters. I missed it. And these girls knew my guys, knew what they were into.

I took the card. There was a little line image of a giraffe on one side and a phone number on the other.

I thought of what my guys had told me, that they were into stealing jewels, and Matteo, the hot, thuggish robot dancer, had once been in their gang. I wondered what kind of disrespect Matteo had shown to get himself kicked out.

Macy Gigi straightened her shirt. "You'll be reconsidering my offer when you figure out your boys are a sinking ship."

What?

The hairs on the back of my neck rose. "Nobody's sinking."

Angel laughed. "Your guys, they're being hunted by the worst people on earth. And how do they respond? Robbing banks in broad fucking daylight. If I had an agency like ZOX after me, I'd be on the moon if I could get there, not in the middle of fucking LA"

She fixed me with a hard look. What was she trying to tell me?

"*Takeover* robberies, Isis. That's the most difficult and fucked-up crime to pull off. They do it because it's high impact, high profile. It's a big fuck you. And I'll tell you something else: it's a death sprint."

I straightened up to my full height, feeling protective of my guys. "They're awesome at bank robbing," I said. "And we're having fun here in LA, so apparently it's not as dire as you think. And we knock over banks with total impunity because we can."

"That doesn't make it smart," Macy said.

"It's smart if you're awesome at it," I replied. "ZOX wishes we were dead. In fact, we're thinking of having that as our motto. We might do a new tattoo." I framed the air just as Zeus had. "You *wish* we were dead, motherfuckers."

Macy smiled. "Yeah?"

I shrugged. "It's an idea we're tossing around. We might have it be on a banner that an angel holds."

Jenny adjusted her breasts inside her slinky white dress, plumping them a bit. Her holster was silver, as was her gun. "Cow-boys. That kind of defiance gets you killed, and that's what they're up to. And also, avenging the doctor. Doctor Thor. It's all about Thor, too. Have you figured that out yet?"

I sniffed all cool and opened my clutch like I was rooting around for something. I didn't like that this conversation was making me feel like I didn't know things about my own gang.

All about Thor? What was that supposed to mean?

What did they know that I didn't know?

I pulled out a chapstick and snapped my clutch shut. "As for death sprint, you couldn't be more wrong. Have you ever been with them on a job? Have you ever eluded agents with them? Any of you?" I looked from one Gigi to the other. "Do you even know the extreme level at which they operate? Are you basing your doom-saying on anything at all?"

The Gigis exchanged glances.

"I'll take that as a no," I said. "I *have* seen them in operation. And I can guarantee you, they've got skills. Nobody's going down. Nobody's crashing and burning. And whoever comes after us will be sorry."

"You're loyal, we like that," Macy said. She snatched the card from my hands and slid it down the bodice of my dress so that it sat against my breast. The cool backs of her fingers brushed against my skin. "If the heat gets too much, or if something happens and you want out, you come around and we'll give you a try on a job. When you're a Giraffe, you can have all the men you want—even manwiches, if that's your thing, but without the side dish of cowboy decision-making. You understand what I'm saying?"

Manwiches? I felt my face heat up.

"And we wear cooler clothes," Angel said.

Macy smiled slowly. "You'll be Ice Gigi." With that, she turned and snapped her fingers in the air. "Gigis."

The two Gigis followed her.

I stared after them, feeling sick. Why would they say my guys were crashing and burning?

I told myself it was just them wanting me to join, but I

couldn't forget that sense of doom that had washed over me in the hotel room earlier—things too bright, too wild.

Also too beautiful.

And thrilling. And I *did* have faith that my guys were the best. And nothing was certain.

I needed to get my guys to start thinking about the future—that's what we needed. Saving their money. Thinking more about safety. A long-range plan.

They deserved more.

I touched up my lipstick and strolled out of the bathroom and around the bar, heading to our table. Thor stood and I slid in next to Odin, who handed me a glass of champagne.

"Thanks," I said.

He reached into the bodice of my gown and pulled out the card. "What's this?"

"I made some new friends in the bathroom."

Odin gave me a dark look, then slid the card to Zeus, who scowled at it.

"The Giraffes aren't anybody's friends," Zeus growled.

"Did they try to recruit you?" Thor asked.

I shrugged. "Not like I'm going to join them."

Odin slammed down his glass. Scotch splashed over the rim. "Those bitches tried to poach you?"

"Who cares?" I said.

"We care," Odin said. "It's an insult."

"It's not like I'm going to join them!"

"What else did they say?" Zeus asked.

"They think you're on a death sprint. That you're going down. Like cowboy outlaws in a shoot-em-up movie." I waited. I wanted to hear what they said to that.

Zeus spoke up. "Do *you* think we're going down?"

"No, I don't think that."

But Zeus heard the hesitation, and a shadow crossed his face.

"We aren't going down. And if we were, we sure as hell wouldn't drag you along with us."

"I know."

"Do you, though?" he demanded.

"I'm telling you what they said."

"You don't know," Zeus said. "And they don't know. We have training nobody else here has. We have skills they couldn't even begin to imagine. You think we wouldn't know if we were going down?" He sat up. "It's because of what happened at your bank, right? Taking you as hostage and getting caught in that jam?"

"I don't think you're going down," I insisted.

Zeus exchanged looks with Odin. "What happened to us with your bank, that kind of thing never happens to us, Isis."

"That was a fluke," Odin said.

I nodded. It's what I needed to hear.

"I can't believe they tried to poach you," Odin said. "They even gave you a card? That shit doesn't stand."

I snatched the card off the table and put it into my clutch. "You need to trust me a little more," I said. "They can try to poach all they want. It doesn't mean I'm going anywhere. They don't say where I go; I say where I go. Got it?"

"Ice," Zeus said. "Hey." Something in his voice pulled on my heart and I looked over to see that vulnerability still there. A kind of pain. "You are always free to leave us if you feel we're going down. You have options. We can make sure you're safe somewhere." Zeus looked so serious and sad saying that.

And suddenly I knew one thing for sure: it cost him to say it.

It was why he hadn't wanted me to join up in the first place, hadn't wanted us to get attached to each other. Because of the idea they might get attached to me, and then I might leave.

"The idea of ever abandoning you guys?" I looked him right in the eye. "Fuck *that*! This is where I want to be," I said. "Did I not, just this morning, get a painful tattoo to prove it?"

"Still. They give you a goddamn business card," Odin grumbled. "I changed my mind. We're hitting the Prime Royale—that will piss off the Giraffes or Gigis or whatever they're calling themselves now."

"Wait, what?" I said. "You were so against it!"

"Now I like the idea," Odin said. "As payback for trying to poach you."

Zeus grinned.

"B-but...the foolishness," I reminded him. "The danger."

"I live for danger," he said. "And I am going to personally grab the Liz Taylor jewels and I am going to wear them around here and watch those bitches stew. I'm going to wear them with something really fucked up."

Thor laughed. "God, it would almost be worth it, just to see you wearing the jewels they always wanted."

"Wait—you, too?" I asked.

Odin was into it. "I'll wear an oily, grimy mechanic's jumpsuit. And these sunglasses. That's what I'll wear them with." Odin smashed the mirrored purple sunglasses farther onto his face. "Yeah, for sure that's what I'll wear with the Liz Taylor jewels. See how *they* like being poached. And we'll grab the Princess Harrod sapphires for Ice to wear. The sapphires are even better than the Liz Taylor jewels." He turned to me, and at that moment, he was irresistible. "You will look amazing in them. We'll wear 'em here. It'll be savage."

Odin seemed unhealthily into this new idea now. Did he honestly want to rob the Prime Royale? I liked a little danger, true. And I loved the idea of Odin and me being outrageous in jewels together. But I was still getting used to this new world—how much danger was too much?

"They liked your tattoo work," I said.

Thor's eyes sparkled. "They like Odin. They like him very much."

"Oh yeah?" I turned to Odin, feeling a pang of jealousy. *They like him?* What did that mean?

"Not like that, goddess," Odin said, brushing my hair from my eyes. "It's a frenemy thing with them. This right here, this is everything. The four of us."

"We can do any bank in our sleep," Zeus said. "Only the Prime Royale is equal to our talents. Every other bank is a cakewalk."

"So true," Odin said. "The Prime Royale is really calling to me now. It'll be a statement to the world. Fuck you, because it's us and Ice all the way."

"Oh, that would be spectacular," Thor said. "The Prime has our name on it. I changed my mind."

Manning was back with the promised gadget. "Tell me I didn't just hear you talking about the Prime."

Odin snorted. "So doing it."

"Why the Prime?" the man asked.

"Because the G's should think twice before trying to poach Ice," Zeus said. "Nobody comes between us and Ice."

"Me and Ice will be wearing those jewels around," Odin said. "It's called a fucking statement."

"Hmm," the man said, stroking his chin, as if to ponder all of this. It was like he was doing a one-man show of pondering. Finally, he spoke. "Is that truly a wise reason to go for the Prime? Petty relationship issues?" He glanced over at me. "No offense, Miss."

I shrugged. I had to agree that it didn't sound like the wisest thing, but I also *did* feel a bit offended. Also, *Miss*?

"Good enough reason for us," Odin growled.

"Well..." Manning tapped the box and headed off.

"It seems unanimous," I said. "On the Prime being a bad idea."

"You need to believe in us more, Ice," Zeus said, sitting up suddenly. "You need to see us in action on a successful robbery. You'll see. Come in with us on First West."

"She's already the driver," Thor said.

"No, she comes in the bank," Zeus said. "We ran without a driver for years. We're hitting it tomorrow."

"Wait, what?" I said. "I'm going to be in the bank? The First West?"

"All you have to do is tag along and stay alert," he said. "You need to see us in a normal robbery. It's the only way you'll understand that there's nothing we can't do," Zeus said. "We're not on a death sprint. The G's are fucked for saying that."

"And we're hitting it tomorrow?"

"Technically, that's today now."

"Seriously?" I said. It seemed a bit soon, but the idea thrilled me, I have to admit.

"Why not? We've been watching it all week." He turned to Odin. "How drunk are you?"

"Not very," Odin said. "Tomorrow-slash-today's good for me."

"We'll hit it when it opens," Zeus said. "But first we need gear. We need outfits. Let's make this one big."

Chapter Twelve

THE FOUR OF US LURKED BY THE BACK DOOR OF THE
Army surplus store under the pale dawn sky, waiting patiently for
Odin to finish picking the lock.

I turned to sit, leaning my head against the wall and staring up
at the morning moon, thoughts returning to my sisters as they had
so often in the past hours and days.

I hoped they were okay. I hoped that they'd get over the death
of me.

Easier said than done.

I reminded myself how resilient they were—I'd seen it when
my parents had died. We four sisters had learned how to reach
down inside ourselves and find that place where we knew things
would be okay. They had it inside themselves to do that again.

I'd had no choice but to allow my death to be staged like it had
been, but it was still awful.

Zeus came over to sit next to me. "They'll be waking up now,
yeah?" he asked.

"Yeah," I said. "A lot of morning chores on a farm."

"So I hear," he said softly.

"I'm thinking that they probably delegated my chores

temporarily between them, but now they'll have to make a permanent shift." *Now that I was dead.* "Hopefully they'll use the money we funneled to them to hire somebody."

"You didn't have a choice," he reminded me.

"I know."

"You saved their lives. It was the only way."

I nodded.

He turned to me then. "If you ever want to talk about it…"

I gave him a weak grin. It was usually Thor who did the sensitive guy stuff. "Thanks."

Odin growled at the lock.

I sighed dramatically and poked Zeus's chest, wanting desperately to change the subject. "All this because *some people* just can't shop like normal folks! Nooooo, our outfits must be stolen."

Zeus snorted. "We like our clothes hot, what can I say?"

"And hot they'll be."

"You know it."

I knew perfectly well why we were doing it this way—so that our purchases couldn't be traced. I checked my phone and sipped my coffee, not that I needed it; adrenaline was surging through my veins like a drug. A robbery before the robbery.

"I can't believe we're going to just *do* this today," I said. "A two-robbery day."

Thor sat down on the other side of me and squeezed my shoulder. His devilish smile told me he knew exactly how I was feeling—wired. Alive. A little bit wild.

We were going to rob a bank in just a couple hours! I felt scared and thrilled, all at once. It was like staring at a sheer rock face just knowing you'll climb it. Thor squeezed again. He felt the same way. We were all thrill junkies in our own ways. These were my people.

The door swung open, and Odin strolled right in, heading toward the alarm box. He yanked off the housing and pulled and twisted the wires, connecting a little box with a keypad.

We walked in after him. The place was hushed and dark, and it smelled like musty cedar. Silent rows of racks held clothes from every kind of military unit. Vintage suits and dresses were arranged on the other side. The walls were adorned with displays, some involving helmets and fatigues, others showing colorful robes and fabrics.

"We'll be back here in thirty minutes, at exactly eight," Zeus said. "No fucking around. Put together some good outfits. Something that allows freedom of movement and plenty of storage. They probably have Halloween masks in the back. Make sure we can see out of them, though."

With that, Zeus and Odin walked out.

The door slammed with a loud *thunk*, leaving Thor and me alone.

Thor smiled devilishly and came to me, stroking his hands up and down over my bare arms, moving his body in close.

Shivers went over me as his chest hit mine. I could feel the steel of his cock through the linen of his slacks. It was hot, us in this forbidden place.

I lifted my hand and stroked his cheek, smoothing over the glint of honey-colored whiskers. I trailed my fingertips over his corded neck.

Crap! I couldn't let myself get turned on. We had a job to do! But the adrenaline was an aphrodisiac to me, and Thor knew it.

"What if the store opens early?" I asked.

"They won't open early. But if they do open, we'd be caught. Maybe we'd have an audience we didn't expect."

I snorted. "Not the best kind of audience."

He kissed my neck, sending shivers skittering over my skin. "Nobody's opening early."

"How do you know?"

"Because this is the kind of information criminals like to have."

I heard a certain something in his voice that I had heard once before—a slight bitterness in how he said *criminals*. He had a thorny relationship with what they'd become—that's the idea that I was getting.

I started thinking here about what the Gigis had said—it was all about Thor. Like Thor was a problem to solve, or like he was a person who needed extra care in some way.

"You're more than criminals," I said.

"Actually, we're less," he said, kissing the base of my throat.

My belly heated with desire.

"It's not what any of us ever dreamed, not even what we trained for," Thor whispered. "We're like goddamn ghosts. We add nothing."

I stepped back. "Stop it, Thor. You guys are awesome."

"We're ghosts of vengeance." He pushed my sleeves partway off my shoulders.

"Thor, I don't want to mess up this job."

"Do you know what it was like, in the restaurant basement tonight? Watching you with them?"

It was technically last night, but I didn't point that out. "We only have half an hour to pick out the costumes. And they said no fucking around."

Thor's voice turned gravelly. "I know what they said."

"They're counting on us."

"Don't worry so much." He pressed close enough that I could feel the heat of his breath on my nose. The electric pulse of excitement between us intensified. "Zeus and Odin are a lot more fun when they're mad. I know you know that."

True enough.

"And it doesn't matter what we do. They're the team. Robbing banks with Zeus and Odin is like if a grade school football team had two professional football players on it. The other players can be terrible, and their team will still win. You and I could do anything, and we'd still be part of the most high-achieving gang on the planet."

He pushed me gently toward a square pillar covered with mirrors and kissed me. He felt so warm and good against me.

"They're the ultimate pros."

I smiled into the kiss. "And you're the doctor."

"Was," he whispered into my ear.

Was? This startled me. Didn't he feel like a doctor anymore? Like he wasn't worthwhile, wasn't a healer?

"You still are. You saved both Zeus's and my lives. What is that, a big zilch? Because it's not a zilch to me. You care. You help people. That doesn't change."

"Shhhh."

The mirror felt cool and smooth on my back, and Thor's kisses were tender and warm.

He said, "I prescribe fucking off a little of this adrenaline. It will help us concentrate."

I pushed him away. "Our job is to get costumes, dude!"

He gave me a dark look; I think he saw that I was serious. Then he smiled, like putting on costumes was a good new sexy idea. "Let's get some costumes on, then."

"Yeah."

I turned to a rack and pulled off a flak jacket. Thor wasn't giving himself enough credit. He was a good doctor and a good man who'd cared enough to speak up when it was hard, when he saw people being hurt and killed, even though it got him into trouble with dangerous people—the dangerous people that Odin and Zeus had once worked for. He was a good robber, too; I'd seen him in action, after all, back when the gang robbed the bank I worked at.

He came up behind me and circled his arms around my waist. "All those pockets in that vest are good. We'll go in really military."

I pointed up at a display on the wall. "Gas masks would be scary."

"They cut off your vision too much."

"I think military is too obvious, anyway. Also, I think it could jinx things because of Odin and Zeus's history. The military wasn't good to them."

"They weren't specifically military," Thor said, smoothing his hands up toward my breasts.

"Whatever. Intelligence ops. Still." I pulled away and walked down a dark aisle. Military boots lined the wall in the footwear section. There were also oddball shoes. I found a rack of wooden clogs. From the Netherlands? I held them up. Thor shook his head. "Impractical for running."

We picked out tall lace-up black boots and tried them on. Comfortable. Thor picked out sizes for Zeus and Odin and put them in the cart. I also found red ski masks. Very classic. They all went in the cart.

"We usually go for more theatrical," Thor said. "Like Halloween masks. It distracts people."

"But if we're covered in black from head to toe and wearing red ski masks, we *would* be theatrical."

"We don't want to look like a mime troupe."

Ignoring him, I grabbed a black long-sleeved shirt and a ragged black military vest with lots of pockets and held them up. "How about these together?"

Thor pulled off his dinner jacket, slowly, and threw it aside. He unbuttoned his shirt slowly, giving me a sexy glower, doing a kind of striptease.

My mouth went dry. "Don't."

"Don't what?"

Don't be so sexy, I thought. *Don't let me see how hot you are when nekkid.*

He threw the shirt and unbuttoned his fly, watching me.

I couldn't look away, and he knew it. I felt like a crazily coiled-up spring, what with the bank robbery in an hour, and here he was, deliciously dangerous, cock straining against the fabric of his black boxer briefs, irresistibly hot and fuckable.

He gave me one of his wicked smiles. "Come here."

"We have a job. One job!" I threw him the rough, black, pocket-laden vest and long-sleeved shirt. "Try that on!"

He put them both on over his black boxers. My resistance was eroding.

"We need pants," he said. "You have one minute to pick out pants."

My pulse raced. If I picked out pants in the next minute, we *would* have time to fuck, which would be fun. Zeus and Odin didn't need to know. But they'd said not to!

Stay strong! I told myself.

I walked deeper into the store, vibrating with excitement, passing silk Japanese robes, trench coats, camouflage fatigues, and more, feeling proud of myself for resisting Thor so well.

I was hoping to find green wool pants. That would be a fun Alpine look—wool pants tucked into the boots.

And then I came to the kilts.

Chapter Thirteen

THOR CAME UP BEHIND ME. "NO WAY."

I pulled a brown and black plaid one off the rack. "Do you know how distracting kilts would be?"

And hot.

I picked out sizes for Zeus and Odin.

"They won't be into kilts," Thor said.

"It'll be perfect. I'm begging you, Thor. Put it on."

He came close, brushed his lips over mine. "What will you do for me?"

"Anything. I will do anything if you wear this."

His eyes darkened. "You already do anything."

"Right now. If you put it on, I'll forget they told us not to fuck around."

"I shouldn't make this deal. I don't see us pulling a job in kilts."

"Let me at least model it for you," I said.

Thor looked wary. Of all the bandits, Thor was the most sensitive to fashion, and I was about to exploit that knowledge.

I really needed this kilt thing to happen. We were about to

walk into a dangerous situation, and if I ended up shot or in jail, I wanted to have my bank robbers in kilts just once.

Also, to fuck Thor while he wore a kilt.

Okay, maybe that was just my libido talking. I pulled off my dress and put on the black boots, so I was wearing only the boots and a thong. Two could play at this game.

Thor licked his lips.

I shook my head and added the black shirt and vest. And then the kilt, in my size. And then slowly, I reached under my kilt and took off the thong and threw it into the cart. "You're not supposed to wear underwear with kilts."

"Jesus." He came to me, kissed me, grabbed my hair. "You have to let me bend you over that crate and fuck you right now," he panted. "I can't believe how hot you are in this thing. You have to let me do that."

My heart raced. "They said no fucking around. Unless you've changed your mind about the kilts. We can fuck if we've finished the task."

He slid a hand up my bare thigh, under my kilt, and pushed between my legs to finger my wet seam. My very wet seam.

I sighed theatrically.

He seemed almost to tremble as he stroked me—I could feel it in his fingers.

The adrenaline of the upcoming job heightened everything.

"Put it on," I whispered. "I'm begging you."

Like he was suddenly possessed by a force beyond him, Thor lurched away and pulled down his boxer briefs, letting his giant golden cock spring free. He pulled on the kilt. With his shaggy blond hair, those massive black boots, the black top, and battle-worn vest, he looked gorgeous and dangerous. Like a post-apocalyptic Scottish ruffian.

Like a god.

I swallowed.

He let me get my fill of him; Thor was diabolical in that way.

Then he came toward me to claim me, locking his hands on my hips. He lifted me onto a tall crate in one fluid motion, and then he kissed me. "I am going to devour you."

"So we're pulling the heist in kilts?" I asked, reaching under the heavy woolen kilt fabric to find his warm, steely cock. I grabbed on to it and let him push into my grip, fucking my hand as I stroked him. I wanted to suck him and fuck him at the same time.

With feverish motions, he pushed up my kilt. I wiggled to let him get it all the way off my ass, even though the crate was slightly rough. I'd never been one to mind rough.

"Is that a yes?" I asked.

"Yes, dammit. Wait." He turned away and grabbed his old pants from the shopping cart and pulled a condom out of the pocket. "Take off your top."

I complied as he rolled the condom onto his cock. Then he grabbed my knees and pushed apart my legs, watching my eyes as he pressed his cock along my slit.

"Thor," I said, taking ahold of his massive girth, guiding him as he entered me slowly and fully, all the way to the hilt in one strong, solid motion.

"Damn," he said, pulling out and thrusting in again.

I felt dizzy and breathless from the exciting and slightly uncomfortable fullness of him.

We panted almost in unison, fucking slow and steady, building up a head of steam. He changed his angle, fucking me new, perfectly rubbing my sensitive nub.

I gasped, consumed with the mounting pleasure of it.

He suckled and bit one of my breasts as he fucked me, and I gasped some more. It seemed so surreal, fucking in kilts right there in a closed store, about to rob a bank. The whole world fell away. There was only his cock pounding into me, his tongue in my ear, on my breast, my hands in his hair.

And the kilt.

"God, Isis," he breathed. "I just want to fuck you forever. This is worth the wrath of Odin and Zeus."

A deep voice behind us. "That's convenient."

Zeus.

Thor froze, mid-thrust.

"Extremely convenient," Zeus continued, "considering that's exactly what you've earned."

I peered over Thor's shoulder. Odin was there in the darkness, too.

"Thor" Odin growled.

Thor didn't bother to crane his neck around. He simply tipped his forehead to my chest, breathing heavily. "You have to let us finish."

"Go out to the car and get the box, Thor," Odin said. "Now."

The box?

Thor looked a little wild as he pulled out of me. He turned and left.

I smoothed my kilt back down and closed my eyes, listening to his boot steps recede, feeling bereft. Odin's box? The paddle? Weren't we on a timetable of some sort? Did we not have a bank to rob? Was the store not going to open?

"What the fuck are you two wearing?" Zeus asked.

"Kilts," I said.

"What the fuck?" he boomed.

"You said to choose an outfit for the job. We chose kilts, and we had a little time to kill..."

"Kilts? This is what you've chosen for us to do the job in?" Zeus grabbed one of the kilts from the cart. Was he angry? "This is what you chose?"

"Yes," I whispered, feeling all screwed up and sexually frustrated—like a bottle of rocket fuel was in me, fully ignited and ready to rocket me to the moon. But with no rocket. And no moon. "It would mean so much to me."

Odin snorted. "You want us to do the job in skirts?"

"They're kilts. Scottish warriors fought whole battles in them," I protested. "Thor said..."

"I bet he did," Odin said darkly. "What face wear?"

"Ski masks," I said. "I know you said not to fuck around, but..."

"Yet you and Thor *did* fuck around, didn't you? Didn't you, Ice?" Odin said.

"Yes," I whispered.

Zeus rummaged through the cart and held up the faded, ripped black vest. "Pockets at least."

"Don't we have a timetable?" I asked, worrying about the box. "And the store will open soon."

"Suddenly that's a concern?" Odin pulled off his jacket and unbuttoned his shirt.

"What are you doing?"

"I'm trying on the costume you're recommending." He began to strip.

"The kilt?"

"It's what you picked, isn't it?" he barked.

Yes.

My belly tightened. Being cut off in the middle of fucking had put me in an absolute frenzy. Now my bandits would all wear kilts? I wasn't sure if my nervous system could handle that.

Odin stripped down to his boxer-briefs and stood there stewing at me. He truly was built like a god, what with his broad shoulders and his thick, lushly muscled chest. My eyes fell to his bulging thighs, the outline of his hard cock. I wanted to feel all of him between my legs. Needed to—bad!

He smiled. He knew.

Another thing I realized: this was only the beginning of my punishment.

And he'd called for the box. The one with the paddle inside it.

Gulp.

He knew I was thinking about that. Also, the danger of the

store clerks coming early—was I the only one worrying about that? They loved to play the edge, my bandits.

Odin pulled the long-sleeved black shirt on over his head. Then he put on the rough, black-pocketed vest. Next, he put on the big motorcycle boots.

Finally, he put on the kilt.

Gasp.

Odin standing there with his mussed hair and his hot, glowery looks wearing beat-up black military stuff with a *kilt* that barely hid his hard cock...he was every sex dream I'd ever had, all combined into a kaleidoscope playing inside my libido.

"Like this, goddess?"

"Yes," I gasped.

His legs were like tree trunks below the hem of the kilt, and god, those motorcycle boots, black and leathery and dangerous.

Not to be left behind in my admiration, Zeus stripped down and put on a matching kilt outfit, and stood before me, all rough and hot and neo-warrior in his own way.

"That's good," I said.

"This is what you're recommending?" He pointed at the cart. "With those red ski masks?"

I swallowed. "Yes."

"This is what you'd have us wear to rob a bank and strike terror into the hearts of those who wronged us?"

"Yes," I whispered.

Zeus cast a dark glance toward Odin.

"What if the clerk comes early?" I asked.

Odin strolled to where I sat on the crate and ran his hands along my thighs, roughly helping himself to me. "*Now* you think about that?"

"Umm...sorry."

"You've been a very naughty goddess," Odin whispered. "Fucking Thor when we said not to."

I could barely see straight at this point, craving more touch, more kilt, more cowbell, more everything.

Odin was rambling on. "...to corrupt Thor like you did. Do you think we can't piece this situation together? Thor wouldn't wear a kilt unless he had a very extreme incentive. And now you'll have to be punished."

"Wait, it's my fault?"

Odin narrowed his eyes. "That's how it looks to me."

"But..." I caught an amused glance from Zeus. "Hold on!" I protested. "Why is it all my fault?"

"Don't worry, Thor will pay, too." Odin touched two blunt, hard fingertips to the side of my face and slid them down, leaving a trail of heat and energy.

The room was quiet as a morgue, aside from the booming of my pulse in my ears, pounding in a rhythm that I could feel clear down to my clit.

He kept going, trailing his fingers on down the side of my neck and farther still, carelessly caressing my bare breasts. "Gods are never fair. We are wrathful. It is in our nature."

It's here I noticed how sped-up his breathing had become. How his eyes shone.

Super into it.

Uh-oh.

His voice went down an octave, sending tremors through my pelvis. "Now get up."

He sounded so serious. Grave, even.

Excitement surged through my veins. "So I get all the blame?"

"And now you get double the punishment, too," he growled. "Any more objections?"

"No," I whispered.

"Good. Now get up or things will get very, very extreme."

I tried not to smile. Could things even *get* more extreme?

"Don't think they can't get more extreme, goddess," he said.

I got up.

He yanked out a different crate and banged it onto the floor right next to the one I was on, creating a kind of bench. He settled himself down on it, right next to me.

"Now bend over my lap."

"What?"

"Shhh, goddess, on my lap. You're getting your punishment early."

"But..."

"But what? The shopkeeper?" Odin glowered. "Well, imagine the scene he'll come upon if you don't *fucking-g* hurry up. Our intelligence says he won't be here for a while, but the longer we stay, the less sure we can be."

I looked down at the kilt covering Odin's muscular thighs—and a boner, I imagined. Suddenly, there was nothing more I wanted in the world than to be over his lap...nothing more except maybe for him to command it again.

"*Now*, Ice."

I stretched carefully over Odin's lap, letting my head hang over the side of the crate, arms and chin resting unceremoniously against the rough pine. I could feel the wood of it on the tops of my breasts, too, just where they hung over the other side of his thigh. I panted, feeling 98% out-of-this-world horny and 2% embarrassed for being so hugely turned on by all this.

I felt masculine hands run up the back of my thigh, pushing up my kilt, baring my ass.

My skin tingled.

My stomach jumped at the sound of a door. Footsteps.

"Thor, show her the box."

Thor, not the shopkeeper. Well, that was good!

Thor's big black boots and kilt appeared in front of me. He kneeled and touched my hair. "Sorry, goddess." He opened the box. A gleaming wooden paddle was nestled into a velvet bed inside.

"Does that look suitable for your crime?" Odin asked from above me.

"We had the costumes all picked out," I said. "I don't see the crime."

"Of disobedience," Zeus boomed.

"Say yes," Thor whispered.

"I guess," I said.

Thor disappeared. The next thing I knew, something cool and smooth tapped once and again on my bare ass—really lightly, just enough to jiggle it. It was so light, it sort of drove me wild. Was this my punishment? To be driven wild with *not enough?*

"How was that?" Odin asked.

I heaved out a breath as he slid the paddle across my bare ass and tapped. I shut my eyes tight. My sex heated. I wanted more...anything.

Zeus pushed Thor away and took his place in front of me. "If the clerks come and open the store, we'll have trouble—because of you two. You are going to learn to obey me in all things. We can't function as a criminal unit without that." His scowl deepened. "Odin?"

I tensed, barely breathing. The silence went on long. Too long.

And then it came—the sting of the paddle on my bare flesh.

I gasped, eyes wide.

Coolly, Zeus said, "One."

Another whack. The slight sting of it blossomed into pleasant sensation, a kind of erotic reverberation.

"Two. Count with me, goddess. Say it."

"Two," I whispered.

There was a whoosh as it came down again, followed by a high-pitched *whap.*

Three. I shut my eyes tight. I felt so exposed—not physically, but about being over a man's knee like this.

"Look at me, goddess."

My breath raced as I gazed into Zeus's green eyes.

Zeus smoothed his hands along my neck and shoulders, caressing me as Odin paddled me. The softness of Zeus's touch and the intense slap of the paddle seemed to link up together inside me, winding inside toward my pussy. Had the spaces between each slap gotten unbearably long? A feeling of pure bliss built inside me, like a cup being filled.

Was I really going to come just from this?

Zeus roamed his hands over me, possessively. "Keep your eyes on me, goddess." His power was sexy and irresistible.

I looked into his eyes. His breath had become as ragged as mine, and I felt like he was reaching into me, filling me, like we were fucking with our minds.

"You belong to us, goddess. We will always care for you, do you understand?"

"Yes," I panted.

"But you and Thor have to obey orders."

"Yes," I said.

"Now, do you want Thor back? To pick up where you left off?"

"Oh, yes," I panted. "God, yes."

Zeus stood.

The paddling had ceased, I realized.

I felt hands caress my stinging butt cheeks and move to my hips, pulling gently upward. "Goddess," Thor whispered. "Up."

Would they really let us fuck now? Or would there be another twist in the punishment? And what the hell time was it?

I crawled a little bit backwards, forearms on the crate, but still over Odin's lap.

Odin closed his fingers over my hair, holding me down against his lap, so that my face was pressed against the rough wool of his kilt. I loved the Neanderthal dirtiness of him holding my hair, pinning me to him. Not like he needed to; not like I was going anywhere. There was nowhere on the planet I'd rather be.

Thor pulled my hips up. "Spread for me, baby," he said,

pushing my kilt up more, sliding his fingers over the tender and probably very pink flesh of my ass.

I widened my stance, melty with desire.

Thor nudged the inside of my thigh. "Open more." I stretched open, and Thor found the entrance to my sex, which was wet, and let's just say yearning.

The tip of his head pressed gently in. I tried to push back, force him in, but Odin held me firmly.

"Please," I said, panting, forehead against the rough, woolly plaid on Odin's lap, fingers clutching his meaty thighs through the fabric.

And then, in one firm, delicious slide, Thor was inside me.

I groaned. I'd waited so long.

Slowly, heavily, he moved in and out. My breath quickened.

"Yes, goddess," Odin whispered, stroking my hair.

The pressure built and built until the feeling of pure bliss expanded and took over my mind. As if that wasn't enough, Thor reached around and slid his clever fingers up and down against my clit and began to stroke.

The sharp, sweet feeling built in me and crested powerfully, like a tidal wave. I cried out as I broke apart in a blinding orgasm that spun on and on. Thor thrust into me again and again, unrelentingly. He pushed fatly into me one last time and grated out a garbled string of profanity as he came.

Sometime later, he collapsed over my back...on Odin's lap.

Best. Manwich. Ever.

With a punishment like this, I thought dizzily, I might disobey more often.

Of course, I didn't actually say that.

"You belong to us, goddess," Zeus said once again.

I looked up, dazed. He was still wearing his kilt. He went and grabbed one of the antique bullet sashes off the wall and put it on over one shoulder.

It was like a Miss America sash, if the Miss America pageant was for hot, dangerous bank robbers who fucked like gods.

"Now let's get out of here, people. Daddy's ready to rob a bank," Zeus said.

We cleaned up. Zeus and Odin switched black face masks for the red ones, and Zeus threw a few hundreds onto the counter.

"That's a high price for what we bought," I observed.

"Wasn't the shopkeepers who put a hit on us," Zeus growled. "Our war is not on the shopkeepers of the world."

Chapter Fourteen

Odin reset the alarm and we headed out into the day, locking the back door behind us. We got into the car wearing our full outfits—the kilts, shirts, vests, and boots. Everything except for the facemasks.

Zeus started up the car and checked his watch before pulling out. "Forty-five minutes."

He and Odin both wore watches, which was unusual for them, but I supposed if you needed to check the time during a heist, you didn't want to have to pull out your cell phone.

I hadn't said anything about the kilts, not wanting to jinx it, but...kilts! Were they really going to wear them for the robbery? With no underwear? I had assumed, from the way Zeus and Odin were talking, that the kilts got nixed and that we'd stop and get different outfits. But they still had them on.

We stopped at a drive-thru and got coffees, then parked in the Valu-Marque supermarket lot across from the bank.

Zeus pulled out binoculars and watched the entrance. "Nobody in yet."

"Wait, so we're just going to do it now?" I asked. "It's time to rob a bank?"

Thor grinned. "It's always time to rob a bank, baby."

"You ready, Ice?" Odin asked. "You feeling okay? If you're not feeling ready, you can drive. We don't want to push you, but we'd prefer you inside. Not just for you to witness our all-powerful skills, but you're ex-bank, after all."

Ex-bank. Because I used to be a teller. I liked that. Zeus and Odin were ex-military and I was ex-bank. "I want to go in. I feel good. Nervous, but good. And not tired at all like I've been up all night," I added.

"You won't be tired 'til after," Odin said.

"So...I thought you weren't going for the kilts," I said.

Zeus lowered the binoculars and directed the full intensity of his gaze at me. "I thought you wanted us to wear them."

"No, I do! I do want you to!"

"Well, I'm getting into them now, too," Zeus said. "I like the easy access. And the way I see it, nothing says *fuck you* quite like robbing a bank in kilts." He glanced back at the bank. "Actually, I'm fucking loving these things. They communicate total disdain to those who have wronged us. It was an inspired choice, Ice. Plus, you think they're hot."

"I do think they're hot," I said.

"There's not a lot we wouldn't do for you, goddess." Zeus said this last bit warmly, humorously, but I felt the gravity behind it, and I recognized it for the deepest kind of truth.

Right then, I understood more than I ever had what the tattoo meant.

We would never leave each other.

We would always care for each other.

We were beyond married.

Zeus put the binoculars back to his face.

We can do anything together, I thought.

"Total disdain," Odin said.

I smiled. "Did you know you're not supposed to wear underwear with them?"

Odin snorted. "Is that public knowledge? That a man is naked under his kilt?"

"Pretty much," I said.

"This just gets better." Odin shimmied off his boxers. "One flash and nobody will be *fucking-g* remembering anything to ID us. We barely even need fake scars and tattoos. They'll be looking at the kilts."

"No, we're still using the disguise stuff," Zeus said. "No need to get sloppy."

Odin grunted and pulled out the little kit. I chose a large thigh tattoo, a scar for my hand, and a beauty spot for my face. We all took a facial mark for luck—and for a mask-off scenario, they called it. Odin had wigs for us all to wear under the ski masks. Thor had grabbed antique bullet sashes for him and Odin back at the store. He put his over his head and across his shoulder.

"I don't get one?" I asked.

"You don't want one, trust me," Thor said. "They weigh a ton."

"But they look cool," I said.

"Right?" Thor raised his blond brows. "They look scary. They look guerilla. Eighty percent of this game is mental."

Odin handed out the guns. My pulse raced as I held mine, a large, silver, semi-automatic of some sort. We'd practiced at ranges, but it was so different to hold a live gun. Zeus and Odin and Thor all had machine guns, though I wasn't supposed to call them that, as well as smaller side arms stuck into various pockets and belts. Things were getting really serious now.

Thor caught my train of thought, it seemed, because he put a hand on my shoulder. "Just to scare people," he said. "We've never shot anybody in the course of a robbery, and we never will. It's not what we're about."

"I know," I said.

"Do you?" Zeus asked. "Because he's right; nobody's getting hurt here. That is the power that we have. Got it?"

I nodded. "I got it," I said.

At twenty minutes to go-time, Odin pulled out a laptop and started hacking into the security firm's site in order to re-route the bank security communications systems. He'd figured out the way in earlier, he'd told me.

Thor pointed at a no-parking hood over one of the meters in front of the bank. "We put that there. One of your jobs will be to cut the ropes and pull that hood off, and then follow us in. You're our helper. Whatever we need, you do it, okay? And the rest of the time, your eyes are on the street and the car, got it?"

I put my hand to my chest. "Got it."

"And we're going to act scary in there," Odin said. "Remember?"

I nodded, recalling that first robbery. Odin had acted particularly dangerous and scary.

"Manager's in," Zeus said. "The tellers will show in a minute or two."

Time seemed to slow. I was starting to feel nerve-jangly. I began to wring my hands, watching people go in and out of the big supermarket on the other side of the street, all having normal days. Unlike me.

"Don't," Thor laid a hand over mine.

"I'm fine," I squeaked.

Odin looked back at me. "Isis. Question: do the woodsmen wear kilts?"

"Excuse me?" I asked.

"You know. In that cartoon porn shit you always watch."

I looked at Odin like he'd lost his mind. I couldn't believe he wanted to discuss my porn predilection at a time like this.

Odin continued. "You know, the woodsmen who capture the helpless elf girl and put her in that stockade?"

"Yes! Stop!" I felt my face heat. "I think I know what you're referring to."

"So do they wear kilts?" he pressed. "Is that the attraction?"

"They wear Robin Hood outfits. Tight pants and hunting stuff. Possibly even tights."

Odin frowned. "Are the tights green? I think of Robin Hood in green."

"I can't believe we're discussing this when we're about to do a heist. I don't want to discuss the woodsmen."

"*Heist*," Zeus laughed. "About to do a *heist*." He seemed to find the word humorous.

"I want to discuss it," Odin said. "A woman's fantasy is fascinating twenty-four hours a day." He wanted to know about the stockade that the cartoon porn woodsmen would place the woman in. He made me describe it in detail. He said they might get some stockades made for their notorious room—just for me. I acted unsure, but eventually I admitted that I'd like it.

We were all laughing by the time Zeus started up the car and pulled out of the lot.

I stiffened.

"Cakewalk," Odin said. "Five minutes. In and out. You cut the meter hood, follow us in, and stay alert. Can you do that?"

"Of course."

"Golden." We put on our wigs, masks, and gloves. The black ski masks were way cooler than the red ones; I loved my bandits for choosing them. I tried to concentrate on that.

We parked at the hooded meter and got out on the sidewalk side. Even Zeus slid over and got out that way. I pulled the box cutter from my pocket, cut the ropes, and yanked the thing off.

Just that made me feel weirdly badass.

I sucked in a breath as I watched my guys slip in. The silver-and-glass door swung closed behind them, flashing bright as it caught the sun just coming up in the east.

Over in the bank window, the open sign went dark. The lights inside went off. My guys were already taking the place over.

I sucked in a breath and headed in.

Zeus was already up on the counter, machine gun in hand,

herding the tellers out onto the floor. "We know all! We see everything!" he yelled. "Try something and you die!" He seemed so scary. And the bullet sash really did perfectly complete the kilt outfit, I thought vaguely.

Thor came near and threw me keys. "Lock up."

I locked the door behind me and turned. My guys were moving with military precision, getting the people under control.

The manager was lying in the middle of the floor with a small handful of customers.

The place was dimly lit now, but you could still make out the slick wood furnishings and metal accents.

Eventually, things were quiet, except for the whimpers of one woman. I wished she understood she didn't have to worry and that we'd be gone in minute.

Right then, everything turned.

Zeus grabbed a lamp off a desk, and with a roar, like a crazed Scottish barbarian or something, he threw it against the wall.

It shattered.

What was happening? Why was he so mad? Somebody screamed.

"All phones means ALL phones!" Zeus yelled.

Odin had his sidearm out—a gun with a silencer. He shot at a man. The man yelped and jerked his arm toward his side. Something black and small exploded into pieces, skittering across the floor.

I gasped. He had shot the man's phone—hopefully before a call had gone through.

"Anyone else want to make a call?" Odin said. "You'll lose the phone *and* a hand!"

Odin turned the gun upward and shot the light, which exploded, showering glass everywhere. You could feel the terror flowing now.

I scanned the street. *Calm*, I told myself. He only shot a phone and a light fixture.

Odin made the people stretch out on their bellies. Then he strolled confidently back to join Zeus, leaving Thor in charge.

When I looked over at Thor, he nodded. Everything cool. I nodded back, keeping my eyes out front.

Odin and Zeus headed back to get the loot.

That's when the trouble started. One of the customers, a middle-aged man, couldn't breathe. He was on his side, gasping.

"I have to help him," Thor said.

I looked at Thor with wide eyes. He was supposed to keep the people in order. Zeus and Odin would kill him if he left his role.

"Fuck me, I can't just stand here," Thor said.

"I know, but—"

"I have to help him." Thor handed me the machine gun. "Hold the crowd."

I stiffened. Hold the crowd? "Excuse me?" I said.

Still in his mask, Thor went to the man and kneeled next to him, loosening the guy's tie. I heard Thor tell the man he was a doctor. He asked about his symptoms. He was no longer using his bank robber voice.

"Call the paramedics, Ice," Thor called.

"What?" I said.

"Just do it."

I pulled out my phone and called 911, reported we needed paramedics at the bank, and that it was a breathing thing. When the 911 operator asked more questions, I just hung up.

Zeus and Odin came out with the manager, loaded down with bags. "What's going on?"

"Respiratory distress," Thor said. "Paramedics on the way."

"What?" Odin barked.

"Okay. We have to leave now," Zeus said.

But Thor was pumping on the guy's chest. "I can't," he said.

"Okay, then," Zeus said evenly. I was shocked at his calm. "Does anybody else here have medical training?" Zeus asked the crowd on the floor.

Nobody had any.

"We have to go," Odin said.

"I can't leave him," Thor said. The man was breathing again, but he seemed very ill. He needed Thor.

"Nobody else? No medical training?" Zeus barked.

One of the tellers raised his hand. "There's a nurse practitioner at Valu-Marque across the street. There's a Zip Clinic there."

"Can a nurse practitioner take over for you, Thor?" Zeus asked. "Would that be acceptable to you?"

"Yup," Thor said. "A nurse practitioner can do this for sure."

Zeus strolled up to me and took my machine gun. "Go get the supermarket nurse, Ice."

"I have to go out there? By myself? What if...what if..." Doomsday scenarios began to crowd my mind.

Zeus lowered his voice. "You're okay, the five-oh isn't here yet. If we have to make a hot exit, you get lost and call us. No matter what happens, we'll fix it. Your safe word means trouble. That's our alert." He watched me levelly, a mountain of strength and calm. "We're good. We can handle paramedics."

"So, I just ask the nurse to uh...to come over here..."

"You need to go in there with a little bit of Odin in you, got it?" he continued. "A little bit Odin and a little bit you. Hear me?" Zeus's gravity centered me. "You can do it. You have nerve and sass. Nobody's more suited."

I nodded. He thought I could do it. It meant everything. And right then, I saw him anew. I saw him as the gifted commander he'd once been.

A little bit Odin. Meaning a little bit scary-bossy. I shoved my gun in my waistband, covered it with my vest and went out, pulling off my mask. I had a blonde, long-haired wig and a beauty mark; it would have to be disguise enough. I ran across the street and slowed when I hit the parking lot. Blood racing, I strolled through the doors.

The environment of the supermarket felt eerily every day-ish, all cheerful lights and muzak. A voice on the loudspeaker alerted me to cinnamon bread being on sale. Carts' wheels squealed. I spotted the Zip Clinic right up front and walked over.

A younger woman was sitting on a stool at the counter. "I'm next," she said.

"Medical emergency." I walked in.

Inside, a fifty-something nurse in a white jacket and dangly earrings stood up from a chair. "You can't just come in here."

The man in the chair looked outraged.

"Medical emergency," I said.

"This isn't an ER," the nurse said.

I felt wild. Desperate. I yanked the man up from the chair. "You have to let me talk to her! You just have to, okay?" He looked bewildered as I pushed him out the door. I think it was my intensity that made him go along with me. Or maybe the wig of wildness.

I closed the door, took out my gun, and pointed it at her with a shaking hand.

The woman's jaw dropped.

A little bit Odin, I thought.

"You can have anything," she said.

"There's a bank customer in respiratory distress across the street. You're gonna come across the street and deal with him."

"What?" She just stared at the gun. "I can't just..."

"Get your stuff or I shoot!"

She just stared at me.

What would Odin do? He'd break something, that's what he'd do. I looked for something to break...but I didn't want to make an alarming sound for the people outside! I swiped a folder off the desk and papers slid across the floor. "Now!"

She looked frozen.

"You want to be on the ten o'clock news for being dead? Or do you want to be on there for being a hero? 'Cause that's your choice now. Get your shit for respiratory distress."

She was still frozen.

I got right into her face and did my best Odin growl. "I am a stone-cold killer and I will shoot this gun right in your pretty face!" I thought the compliment might soften things, but when I heard myself say it, not so much. "Do it!"

Her lip quivered. "Please, no!"

I grabbed a bag and put it over my gun. "Get your breathing stuff or that guy across the street won't be the only one who needs it!"

She sprang into action, grabbing a large Tupperware box.

"Go. Eyes forward," I said in the scariest voice I could muster. "And if you signal anyone, I'll see it and I will *so* shoot you. I see all! I am a fucking cyclops!"

She grabbed a box of latex gloves while I remembered a cyclops only has one eye.

"Also, I'm a satellite, watching from every direction. The point is, you better act natural." I opened the door and we headed out.

"Be right back," she chirped to the man and the woman waiting. We beelined out as a pair, down the parking lot, and across the street. I felt like a total asshole.

The bank was still dark. I pushed open the bank door and ushered her in. She went to the man's side. Thor turned to her and started talking. She pulled something out of her box. They were working together now.

Sirens sounded in the distance.

Cops? *Was this it?*

My blood raced.

"Thor," Zeus said.

The sirens grew louder.

Everything seemed to move in slow motion.

"One sec." Thor ripped open a pack. The nurse took over the pumping. I couldn't see what else they were doing.

"No more time," Zeus said.

My heart pounded.

Thor stood. We walked out of the bank slowly. The street looked normal, but the ambulance was down at the end. There were more sirens now, coming from the other side, it sounded like.

"Crap. Cops," Zeus said, pulling off his mask. We all followed suit, pulling off our masks as discreetly as possible. "Easy, everyone."

We opened the doors to the van and slid in with our bags, Thor and me in the back, Zeus and Odin in front.

"Let's get out of here!" I said.

"It's okay, we're good," Zeus said. "Down, everyone. Hide."

Thor and I huddled down so that nobody from outside could see us. Up front, Odin did the same. My pulse drummed in my ears.

Zeus started up the engine and pulled out just as the windows lit up red. I couldn't believe how slowly he was going.

A siren blasted—it sounded like it was right next to us.

"Fuck," Zeus said.

"We okay?" Thor asked.

"Not yet," Zeus said.

"I couldn't leave him," Thor grated. He sounded so strong about it. He couldn't leave the man.

I wondered if he would be in trouble now for real. He had nearly messed up our escape. He stared at the seatback. He looked determined and strong.

And strangely, calmer. That weird energy I'd been feeling off of him all week was gone. What had changed? Was it having the chance to act like the doctor he was after so much time? Was that it?

I thought about the reckless joyride Thor had taken me on during those early days, him wanting to shoot down the dolphin sculpture, and getting Zeus riled up at the massage place. Pushing against the confines of the group. Was that Thor, pushing against the limits of our life?

I studied him harder, and I caught another hit of that new

serenity in him, and when he looked up with that cool blue gaze, I knew that was it. Being a healer was a deep part of his identity, and he'd been cut off from it for way too long,

"I know. I get it. You had to help him," Zeus said from up front. "I understand."

Thor nodded.

"Steady," Odin said.

The sirens sounded louder and the windows flashed red. I thought about a hot exit, which meant exactly what you might imagine—going out with guns blazing.

It was definitely cooler to talk about a hot exit while you were lounging in your hotel suite eating bon-bons than when you were riding in an SUV loaded with guns and money while cops prowled the streets around you.

Thor reached out and took my hand and squeezed it.

I squeezed back. "What's up, doc?" I said.

He rolled his eyes but didn't let go of my hand. I was glad for that. I needed that contact with him just then.

We held hands like dorks there in the back seat, gripping onto each other for a very tense five minutes as the vehicle crawled through the streets.

And then another five minutes. More time passed. We turned again. Again.

"Unmarked car on our tail," Zeus growled.

Thor muttered a curse under his breath. I closed my eyes.

"Odin, can you do something with the traffic lights?" he asked.

"Not from down here. I'm plotting a route, though," Odin said.

The sirens were sounding fainter.

"This guy tailing us, he's suspicious," Zeus said. "Getting more so. Really looking at us."

"He's probably just seeing what we'll do," Odin said from his crouched position in the front.

"He's going to pull us over," Zeus said. "He sees these kilts and we're done."

"Sorry," I said.

"The kilts fucking rocked," Zeus said.

"Make a U-turn at the next light," Odin said, monitoring the situation from his super-military maps app, no doubt. "If he follows, we run, and I've got a route."

I felt queasy as the hulking vehicle swung around.

"Is he following?" Odin asked.

"Yup," Zeus said.

Crap. My blood raced. Was this it?

"Step on it," Odin said. "You'll take a sharp left on Oak."

"Wait," Zeus said.

"Do it," Odin barked.

"He put on his signal," Zeus said.

"Don't chance it," Odin warned. "It could be a fake-out. He wants us past Oak."

I held my breath. The seconds stretched.

"Zeus," Odin warned.

"He's turning," Zeus said.

"You sure?" Odin asked.

"Yes!" Zeus hissed out a breath. "We're good."

I heaved out a sigh of relief.

We had to stay down for a long time after, but when Zeus finally gave the A-okay to sit up, I threw myself at Thor and hugged him. "We're okay," I said.

He held me tight, pressed his face onto my shoulder. "We're okay," he whispered. And then, to the group, he said, "I'm sorry."

"We can't take you anywhere, can we, Thor?" Zeus joked from the front. But it was one of those tiny-bit-of-truth jokes.

"He would've died," Thor said.

"I know." Zeus eyed Thor in the rearview mirror. He lowered his voice like he did when he was talking really seriously. "We're a family now. You know what family means? We get to mess things up and be messed up, and we still belong together. You won't be rid of us, even if you act like the biggest screw-up in the world. And vice versa. We're all stuck in this thing, and I know you've felt restless, like this isn't the life you set out for yourself. But you know what? There are no rules to what we have to be. You had to save that guy. It was the most important thing to you right then, so you know what? It was the most important goddamn thing to me, too."

"And me," Odin said.

"Me, too," I said. "It needed to happen."

Thor nodded, taking it in.

"The God Pack should never be a prison or an authority," Zeus said. "We're a creative fire supporting each other to be whatever the fuck."

Odin grunted in assent. "Yeah, we're a creative *fucking-g* ferment."

"Yeah. A creative ferment. Okay?" Zeus said.

"I got you," Thor said.

I nodded, unsure what *ferment* meant when used as a noun, but it wasn't the kind of moment where you wanted to pull out your phone.

"And you know what else?" Zeus asked. "We're going to find some more doctoring opportunities for you, and that's final. And I don't mean patching bullet wounds for jackasses who get themselves shot. Real doctor stuff."

"I don't see how," Thor said. "I don't have privileges anywhere."

"We'll figure it out," Zeus barked. "We're getting you doctoring again, got it?"

"Thank you," Thor said. "Thank you." He definitely seemed calmer. More settled. He'd needed to express himself as a doctor the same way I'd needed to bust off of that farm and challenge myself, find the edge of myself.

I thought about the way Zeus had seemed to peer into my

soul back in the army surplus and vintage store. I had a new sense of him, of all my guys. We made each other more whole, I realized.

"Even so, it wasn't fair to you all," Thor said.

"It's not about fairness," Odin said. "It's about family."

Maybe it was my highly emotional state, but tears stung my eyes. There were no limits to what we would do for each other.

I looked over at Thor. I don't know how Zeus thought he could get him doctoring again, but together, we could do anything.

I leaned up and half hugged Zeus—as much as you could from the back seat while a guy was driving, anyway.

He ruffled my hair, like it was all so casual, but the tenderness in his eyes tore a hole in my heart.

I moved over to sort-of-hug Odin, clutching as much of his chest as I could reach, and then I kissed his shoulder.

"Goddess," he said, like it was a little bit unnecessary, but he rested his arm over mine and squeezed me back—hard—like he needed it as much as I did.

We were okay for now.

Zeus said, "Odin, tell me every fucking camera in that supermarket was off, or else Ice is everywhere on TV tonight."

I'd almost forgotten. I had gone into that supermarket with my mask off.

"I took their cameras offline, too, like you said," Odin said. "Unless one of the shoppers was filming."

"Yikes," I said.

"Why would they?" he said. "From the sounds of it, you were cool as a cucumber."

"I was a fucking cyclops," I said. "A cyclops in a satellite."

"Umm...yay?" Thor said.

"So, is the guy gonna be okay?" Odin asked.

"I think so," Thor said. "He was stabilized. That nurse knew her shit."

"You needed to help him. We needed you to do that," Zeus said. "Case closed."

Odin was rooting through one of the bags. He pulled out a bundle of money. "Dye packs." He tossed them out the window.

Luckily, we still had a ton of money left. A ton!

"That was—" I put my hand over my thundering heart. "Oh my god—we did it!"

Odin smirked. "Anybody can rob a bank when the robbery runs smoothly. What sets us apart is that we can handle the complications. And if it had come to a hot exit, we would've handled that, too, because we have the tactical advantage in every way, not to mention the *motherfucking-g* balls to pull it off."

I smiled, loving Odin and his bank-robbing prowess. They all seemed to be looking at me, waiting for me to add something. I sat back and crossed my legs. "The Giraffes obviously don't know shit about us. We kick ass, and always will!"

"Hell yeah," Zeus said.

I chuckled. "And when they see we knocked over a bank in kilts, they are going to shit."

"So is Agent Denko," Odin said. "Denko will shit."

"You think he'll know it was us?" I asked.

"Defo," Odin said. "Especially with Thor's stunt. But with no new images? We're fine."

For now—that was the unsaid part of it.

Would their mortal enemies ever let them just live? Would they ever let them just be? Right then, I realized, if I could have any wish, it would be that—for my guys to live in peace. Never to have to look over their shoulders. They didn't seem to care about that as a goal, but it was officially my goal now.

"You *wish* we were dead, motherfuckers," Zeus said. "That goes on the tattoo."

I groaned.

"Let's do it," Zeus said. "Another tattoo!"

"Where to now?" I asked. I was feeling starved and wired and exhausted, and even a little horny.

"Home, goddess," Thor said. "Home."

For a second, I imagined the farm, but of course that wasn't possible. My thoughts flew to my sisters as they had so often since the decision to kill Melinda. I whispered a little prayer out to the universe for them to heal quickly from the loss of me. For them to stun everybody with the power of their optimism and embrace of life. For them to know, somewhere deep inside their hearts, that everything was okay.

No, I wouldn't be going back to that farm anytime soon. It was their home they meant. The hideout they'd told me so much about.

"Are you sure?" I asked. "What if they're watching it?"

"We're reasonably sure that ZOX doesn't know about this one. Our surveillance guy, Manning—the one you met at Guvvey's? He checked it out," Zeus said.

I nodded. "The weird brocade jacket guy with the one-man pondering show?"

"He's weird, but one of the best," Zeus said.

"ZOX will think we've blown town," Odin said. "Just wait."

A small grin crept onto Thor's face. "Right, because what would be more ridiculous than staying in town after such an ostentatious robbery? And doing one that's even wilder?"

"Right?" Odin said. "And anyway, I have somebody scattering breadcrumbs out in Maine. That will keep them busy for a while."

"Maine would be a logical place to go. Seashore?" I asked.

"Of course," Odin said. "You know how we like a lot of escape routes."

"Home, then," Zeus said.

Home. Was it too good to be true? And what about the Prime Royale? Even their own surveillance guy had warned against it. I thought again about his one-man pondering show. Was he just a freak, or was he scared to come right out and tell them the truth?

MY BANDITS' HIDEOUT WAS A GLASS AND STONE building nestled into a hill behind a thick cover of trees, and if you looked hard, you could catch sight of the ocean beyond.

The interior was full of colorful furniture, modern art, and books. Fanciful lanterns hung from the ceiling, and a strip of flame burned behind blue glass.

I'd never seen such a fireplace, such a home. It was comfortable, and more whimsical than I'd imagined, too. Odin had picked out the stuff, of course.

Zeus showed me my room. It was simple and elegant with a view of the sun-splashed ocean through the trees. "You go ahead and make it yours however you want," he said. "That was a rich haul. You'll see when we split it."

"It'll definitely need a Paris Hilton sheep's wool comforter," I said.

"We'll all get one."

I settled in and put a few things away. I was excited to be able to put my clothes in a dresser and know they'd be there for more than forty-eight hours.

I'd never even had a room of my own.

Back at the farm with my sisters, I shared a room with Vanessa.

After I'd settled in, I headed back out to the main room to find Thor going around flinging open windows. Zeus was downstairs getting in a quick workout.

I grabbed a snack and settled in with a book.

Home.

There was a hot tub, of course, and the remnants of a garden Thor had planted the year before. It seemed that they came here on and off when things felt safe.

We grilled a late dinner and slept like logs, or at least Thor, Zeus, and I did. You never knew about Odin. He had such sleeping issues, sometimes even thrashing around. Maybe settling down for a spell would help him.

The next day was the ultimate fun—nothing extravagant, nothing scathingly sexy, just the simple fun of playing house with three amazing guys.

Thor got up ridiculously early and snagged coffees and an actual old-fashioned newspaper, and the four of us sat out on the deck and read it, passing around the different sections like people in old movies.

Later I washed dishes with Zeus to some 80s hair band that he wanted me to hear. Even that felt special.

I guess there's nothing like constant danger to make you appreciate everyday things.

The porch overlooked a hillside of trees and homes, sloping down to the ocean that was wild with whitecaps. It was like being in a treehouse with the hottest guys alive.

One of the things we confirmed from the newspaper was that the man in distress would be okay. He was recovering well.

Thor had really and truly saved him.

The other good news was that none of the supermarket shoppers had gotten my picture. It looked like all they had was a bad sketch of me, complete with wig and the beauty mark.

But, oh my god, this sketch! Even my sisters wouldn't recognize me. I barely recognized myself. There were sketches of Thor, too, but they weren't as bad.

"It's like they tried to make me look as dorky as possible. What's with my cheeks? And my nose? And I don't have lopsided eyes!"

Zeus just laughed. "Be happy that it doesn't look like you!"

"I know, but I feel like they're trying to troll me."

Later that day, Zeus got into doing some repair work on the deck. I loved that he was so handy. The ultimate in competence porn, my Zeus.

Thor went out and started weeding his garden; we might not be there to see it grow, but Thor cared about things like that.

Odin enlarged the sad images of us and printed them off and colored them in like Andy Warhol pictures. I wasn't so sure about this art idea, considering my lopsided eyes and horror show nose, but I loved that it was such a fuck-you thing to do.

"How long do you think we can stay here?" I asked him while he cut mats.

"I'm hoping for a few weeks," he said. "But who knows, maybe longer. Ideally long enough to plan and execute the Prime Royale job."

They were talking about bringing Matteo in on it now. It would be like a bank robbery supergroup.

Odin finished his masterpieces, eventually. He hung them on the wall above the blue flame fireplace and called Thor and me in to see.

We gushed over them, possibly embarrassing Odin, but he really had created something wonderful.

"I will admit that I was skeptical," I said, "but now I love them!" I turned to Thor. "You look especially notorious."

Thor grinned. "And you look especially sassy!"

I hugged Odin. "Best. Most wanted pictures. Ever."

"Enough," Odin growled. "Who's hungry?"

"I am," Thor said.

"So so," I said.

Odin yelled the question down to Zeus, who boomed back an enthusiastic *fuck yeah*!

I snorted. My guys were always hungry, and not just the sexy kind of hunger. Dudes will pretty much always eat; this was a new and amusing thing that I definitely hadn't experienced growing up in a home full of girls.

Odin looped an arm over my shoulder. "I'm gonna suggest an appetizer of almond croissants and then…Thai?"

"Thai and pizza," Zeus said, bounding in.

"Good with me," I exclaimed.

Thor grabbed the keys. Another thing I'd learned is that outlaws rarely order delivery food, which made a lot of sense. Just take-out.

For our first stop, we headed into croissant express. My bandits picked out a selection of croissants while I teased them about having dessert before dinner.

"Always, goddess," Thor said with a wink.

I rolled my eyes. "I would insist you eat something wholesome first."

"Is that right?" Thor said as we made our way out the door and back to where our shiny SUV was parked. "What did you have in mind?"

I had backseat hijinks in mind, to be perfectly honest, but just then, Zeus let out a string of profanity, and Thor gripped my arm —hard—stopping me in my tracks.

Zeus and Odin both had their weapons out, hanging discreetly down by their sides, and were moving ahead, or more melting slowly ahead, disappearing into the row of cars parked along the street.

"What's going on?" I whispered to Thor, pulse pounding. Had ZOX caught up to us after all?

"Check out the windshield," he said.

I squinted in the bright sun, and then I saw it—a scrap of paper stuffed under the windshield wiper.

"Maybe it's an ad for a carwash," I said.

"Then why isn't there one on every car?" Thor grumbled.

"Oh," I said.

Thor and I backed up to lean against the rough stucco wall outside of the bakery, scanning the scene while we waited for Zeus and Odin to attend to their project of skulking invisibly around the row of cars along the street.

What they clearly weren't attending to was reading the note, because it was just sitting there still on the windshield. I was burning with curiosity at this point.

"Maybe it's nothing," I said. "Maybe it's a carwash ad, but everybody else who got it drove away. Wasn't Odin saying just last night that the ZOX guys were supposed to be poking around in Maine? They have no idea that we're here."

"When you're in hiding, no note's a good note," Thor said.

"Shouldn't they just read it?" I asked.

"They will," Thor said. "Whoever left the note is probably lurking around, so that's the focus now. The note will be there."

We waited for what seemed like forever, scanning the street from our post against the wall.

Ten minutes later, Odin appeared next to the SUV. He nodded at us, and Thor nodded back.

Odin plucked the paper from the windshield and shook it gently to unfold it, holding it by the corners and studying it with a frown.

Zeus went over next to him, and they both studied it. Zeus took a picture of it.

"Suspense definitely building," I said. "Will they be coming over and showing us anytime soon?"

"Right?" Thor said. "What the hell."

"Can't we go over there?" I had no doubt that Zeus had thoroughly checked the SUV for bombs by now.

"Let them do their work," Thor said.

Sigh.

Finally Odin was heading back toward us. He nodded as he passed and went right into the bakery.

"Hello," I mumbled. "Any day with the note."

Thor snorted.

"Or was this just an elaborate excuse for more croissants?"

"I wish," Thor said.

Odin came back out with the note in a plastic bag. "Come on," he said.

I pushed off the wall and followed him and Thor back to the vehicle.

Zeus nodded at the dry cleaner that we'd parked in front of. "I'm gonna go in there and see if they saw who dropped this. If anybody saw anything, it'll be these guys."

"Agreed," Odin said. "I'll try that deli. Can you two maybe Google that shit? I airdropped the image to you."

Thor and I took out our phones. Sure enough, we each had an image of the note. I clicked on it and opened it up. The note began with the words "TAKE HEED," written in loopy cursive. The rest of it was a typewritten passage several sentences long.

Passion has helped us, but can do so no more. It will in future be our enemy. Reason, cold, calculating, unimpassioned reason, must furnish all the materials for our future support and defence.

"Well, if this is a car wash ad, it's a shitty one," I said.

"No shit," Thor said.

I typed the text into a search bar and got my answer instantly.

"It's the second to last paragraph of Lincoln's 'Lyceum Address,' given in January of 1838—when he was twenty-nine."

"Weird," Thor said.

"I know, right? Can you imagine a twenty-nine-year-old of today saying anything close to this? Like coming up with even one of these sentences?"

"No, I mean it's weird as a note that somebody would send to somebody like us," he clarified.

"Yeah, that too."

"It reads like a warning," Thor said. "Don't you think?"

"*Take heed* definitely suggests a warning. But a warning about what? Too much passion?" I frowned. "Wait, should I be insulted?"

"You do inspire a great deal of passion, it's true," Thor said. "But passion comes in many forms. It could be a warning about getting too riled up about anything."

I nodded. Thor didn't say it, but I suspect he was talking about Zeus here, the way Zeus could get carried away about things. But then, Thor was no great shakes in the unimpassioned reason department, let's just say, considering that he'd almost gotten us caught with his passion for saving lives. It was a great passion to have, obviously, but it had put us in danger. Could that be the warning?

"What were the circumstances of the speech?" he asked, interrupting my train of thought.

I scanned the Wikipedia article. "The speech was given before Lincoln held any kind of office. It's a warning about tyrants, basically."

"Hmm," Thor said.

"I think the only tyrants in our lives are ZOX," I said.

"Agree," Thor said.

Zeus was back. "They did see something. A guy dressed as Abe Lincoln in a top hat and beard. And black gloves," he added.

Thor frowned. "Gloves."

"Yup," Zeus said. "We'll see if we can lift prints, but when I see gloves..."

"Unlikely we get anything."

"The Lincoln get-up does make sense," I told him. "The passage is from an early speech that Lincoln gave at some kind of young men's club." I related what I'd learned.

Zeus glared down at my phone. "Take heed," he said. "So it's a warning."

"A warning against tyrants," I added.

"What the fuck," Zeus seethed.

Odin sauntered up. "There's a performance art group in the neighborhood. The deli clerks said that sometimes they go around dressed as clowns putting up weird signs on lampposts, and they *have* put screeds under people's windshield wipers in the past. The clerk said that he got a drawing of Ronald McDonald under his windshield wiper one time. When I told him about the Abe Lincoln character, he was sure that he would have come from the group."

"Then why are we the only ones who got it?" Zeus asked.

"Maybe everybody else drove away? Or maybe randomness is the point," Odin said.

I had my handy Wikipedia article open. "By some definitions, the goal of performance art is to generate a reaction." I looked up. "They would get more of a reaction if it's just one person that gets the note, because it seems more specific."

Zeus sighed. "I'm getting a fucking reaction alright. I assume you got their address."

Odin had an address. I plugged it into my phone, and we headed off, around the corner to a sad office building with a facade of cracked stucco and bars on a large and very dirty ground-floor window. You couldn't see into the window because there was a thick curtain covering it, but it had once been a storefront from the looks of it. A small, hand-written sign was taped to the corner of the window with one word: Irony. Some kind of music was coming from in there, hypnotic and grungy.

Zeus rapped hard on the metal door.

No answer.

I was feeling despondent. Was our fun going to be over so soon? Our wonderful life at the hideaway?

Zeus knocked again; still nobody came to the door. Odin sighed and pulled out a small leather wallet-looking thing that I happened to know was one of his lock-picking kits.

"I so hope it was them," I said as Odin worked at the lock. "Let it be just nothing. Just a weird freak thing."

Thor sighed. "Unlikely, goddess."

A loud click signaled that Odin had cracked the lock.

Right then, the door was yanked open from the inside, and we were face-to-face with a large man with chunky black glasses, purple hair, and a short, immaculately trimmed beard. "What the hell are you doing?" the man barked.

Zeus showed him the bag with the note in it. "This yours?"

The man studied it with a frown. "No."

"Let me rephrase that," Zeus said. "Did you or anybody you know put this on our windshield?"

"Fuck no." He gave it back. "And this shit?" He pointed to the lock the Odin had opened. "Next time I call the cops."

He tried to shut the door, but Zeus shoved a foot in the way.

"That's it, I'm calling now." The man had his phone out. Odin plucked it from his fingers.

"Hey!"

"Look, we really are sorry to bother you," Thor said, taking a polite tone. "We were just extremely upset to see this strange warning, and we're trying to get to the bottom of it. Are you sure it doesn't seem familiar? Or like the work of somebody that you might know?"

"Lemme see it again," the man said.

Thor handed the bagged note over.

The man scowled at the thing. "This was on your windshield?"

"Left by a man dressed as Abe Lincoln," I said. "It's an Abe Lincoln speech fragment."

"Take heed," the art dude said. "Looks like somebody is giving you a heads up on something."

"You sure this isn't somebody from your group?" Thor asked. "You and you group have put things on windshields before."

The man sniffed, insulted. "Maybe so, but I promise you—this? No. Zero chance. Precisely zero. I mean, seriously? A few lines of a speech by Abe Lincoln delivered by a man dressed as Abe Lincoln. How stupidly literal is that? If we had any interest in delivering Abe Lincoln speeches around town—and I guarantee that we do *not*—but if we did, we wouldn't dress as Abe Lincoln. We'd go with something like a clown or a large rabbit or...maybe not that but..."

"Why?" Zeus asked.

"Because we'd want to add something new. Some kind of juxtaposition or commentary or if nothing else, a nonsensical element. Otherwise, what's the point?"

I nodded like I got it, but I didn't see the point of any of it.

Odin, apparently, was fully following along. "Couldn't Abe Lincoln coming from the past to deliver warnings about tyrants to be some kind of commentary on the present?"

"We're not political like that, but even if we were, it's too on the nose," the man said. "Because you already have Lincoln in the speech. So, Abe Lincoln delivering part of an Abe Lincoln speech? Why would anybody waste their time stupidly echoing an element that's already present? As performance art, it's idiotic."

Odin nodded. "Agreed."

"Thank you," the man said, seeming both highly annoyed, but grateful that Odin got it. "A thing like this...wait—lemme see that note again."

Thor handed it over.

Zeus looked hopeful. "Got something?"

"Maybe," the man said, examining it. "Hold on," he added.

Did he have an idea? Did he recognize the handwriting? The style?

We held on. Maybe this could still be easy. We'd find out it's nothing, go get our takeout food, and have a nice night.

"Yup," the guy finally said.

"Yeah?" Odin asked hopefully.

"They should've dressed as one of monkey dudes from *Planet of the Apes*." He looked us expectantly. "As a counterpoint? That would've been a comment."

"Fun!" I said, just because the guy seemed so into it.

Thor took the note back. "Thank you."

"Okay, then," Odin said, handing back his phone. "How many people are in your group?"

"Fifteen, thirty...depending. It's not like we're the Shriners."

"But people in the public know about you. They know that you operate in this area," he pursued.

"Sure. And we put out the word when we're going to do an action. We're on TikTok."

"You know what I think it is?" Thor turned to us. "It's somebody trying to make it *look* like this guy delivered us a note."

"So we look like idiots?" the artist grumbled.

"It's not about you," Thor said. "It's a message for us. My guess is somebody knows something, but if they specifically warned us, it would put them in danger. So they deliver a generic heads-up. Be wary. Something's coming."

"Dressed as Abe Lincoln, though?" Odin said. "Why not just make a fake yahoo address and email us?"

"Or hello. Hat and sunglasses, anybody?" I said. "Why frame the artist gang?"

"Hold on..." Thor held up a finger. "What's the difference between an email directed at us and a note left for us by an art group that likes to leave random notes for people?"

"The randomness?" I tried.

"Right," Thor said. "It's somebody wanting to deliver a message to us, but they want to make it look random."

"Why?" Zeus fumed.

"Well, uh..." The artist winced. "You did break into a guy's home in broad daylight. Maybe the person is scared?"

Odin glared at him. "We gotta go."

"You sure you can't stay?" the man asked. "This is getting interesting."

Odin gave the artist a small stack of bills. "A donation for your next show. We were never here."

We headed out.

"He really wanted us to stay," I said once we were on the road. "He liked us."

"Or we end up as his next art project." Odin glared at passing signs. "They wanted to make the message *feel* random. But obviously we'd investigate."

"The person wore gloves," Zeus observed. "They're probably in the system. I bet it's someone from Guvvey's. It's not exactly a well-balanced crowd."

"Why be so extra?" Thor said.

We picked up our pizza and Thai food and headed back home.

Over dinner, we discussed all the ways somebody could've pulled the whole thing off. Did they follow us? Did they lurk at the croissant place? Did they carry the costume around, waiting for their chance?

And was the note designed to screw with us? Or help us?

The discussion went in circles. Twisted into pretzels. It headed into dead ends.

Zeus threw his napkin onto his plate. "All this confusion. Not loving it."

"Maybe this is a sign to re-think the Prime Royale," I tried.

Odin groaned. "Jesus, that's it! Psy-ops 101. Confusion disrupts an adversary's decision-making process."

"Excuse me?" I said.

Zeus perked up. "Somebody wants us to steer clear of the Prime Royale."

"Could it be the G's?" Thor asked. "It's not their style, but they do want what's in that bank."

Odin nodded. "Somebody else has their eye on the Prime Royale. Are you guys thinking what I'm thinking?"

"I'm probably not thinking what you're thinking," I said.

Zeus said, "Somebody's trying to spook us off of the Prime Royale because they want it for themselves."

"This makes me even more excited to hit it." Odin rubbed his hands.

"With a big enough haul, I could fund some shit. I could start a clinic somewhere."

I groaned.

"It's gonna be amazing," Thor said. "Somebody trying to scare us off. Such bullshit!"

"This isn't an episode of Scooby Doo," I said. "It's real life, and warnings should be heeded. Think about what happened at the First West."

"That only confirms that we should do it," Thor said.

Odin pointed his fork at me. "We fucked up in every way on the First West job and we still made off like the world-class operators that we are. Thor stopped to do an entire medical procedure, you trotted across the street and took a hostage, and it all worked out. Don't you see? That experience is more powerful than any warning, and more meaningful than some dickish note delivered by fake Lincoln. Somebody wants to warn us away from living wild and free? Away from passion? Away from the biggest haul of the world? Fuck that! We'll rob the Prime Royale in such a blaze of passion that the *fucking-g* sun will fall out of the *fucking-g* sky."

Zeus grunted. "What he said!"

"Oh my god." I set down my fork and covered my face.

"Come on, Ice!" Odin said. "We are the most badass robbers; it's only right that we should rob the most badass bank."

"I believe in our awesomeness, but I want us to be safe."

A big, warm hand wrapped around my wrist, tugging gently. Zeus.

I allowed him to pull my hands from my face.

"With the First West, you were amazing," Zeus said. "You've got nerve, Ice. You can easily sit with the getaway car and drive. If things get hot, I'll take the wheel."

I imagined driving through a hailstorm of bullets—that's the kind of *hot* he meant. "You taking the wheel would probably be best in that scenario," I said.

"But it's up to you if you're in or not," Zeus said.

"Completely up to you," Odin said.

"We won't do it if you don't want to," Thor said.

I looked at my guys, feeling so much love. They'd let me decide?

I couldn't stop thinking about that warning, of course.

Was it a message from the universe?

A random ripple on the surface of our life?

Or a specific warning from a person who knew us?

And if it was the latter, did that person want the Prime Royale for their own, or did they have some special knowledge of danger we faced?

But then, weren't we always facing danger? What was so new about that? Whoever was behind the mysterious warning, we would deal with them.

When the world said no, we said yes.

We said *fuck yes.*

I smiled. "What kind of dipshits change bank robbery plans based on an Abe Lincoln quote?"

Thor grinned. "Yeah, baby!"

Zeus pulled me from my chair and twirled me around.

Odin announced that he was going to start designing our new tattoo with our new motto, *You WISH we were dead, motherfuckers.* "With angels and scrolls and shit."

I laughed about this new tattoo idea. It was *so* Odin.

So *us*.

The four of us were just a little bit in love with each other, and it was a very good day to be alive.

~ The End ~

Thank you so much for reading *The Wrong Idea*!!!! I hope you love and cherish the gang as much as I do.

&

But wait...is the danger truly past?

Question: What happens when a stalker leaves creepy, threatening gifts for Isis?

Answer: ZOMGGGGGGGG

Isis always knew her bank robbers were ruthless and brilliant.

After all, they take their names from gods. They've eluded law enforcement across the globe. And with just the crook of a little finger, they're able to bend her to their every forbidden desire.

But it isn't until Isis gets a creepy stalker that she realizes just how dangerous her guys are.

The stalker's threats unleash the robbers' most primal and possessive instincts as they blaze a path of destruction through the criminal underground. But is it too late to save her?

Find out in THE DEEPER GAME, available at your fave bookseller.

DANGEROUS ROYALS

Dark and edgy mafia romance; read in order

Dark Mafia Prince

Wicked Mafia Prince

Savage Mafia Prince

Annika Martin writes in many genres; find a complete list of her books, audiobooks, and translated works at www.annikamartinbooks.com

All the Annika deets!

Annika Martin is a New York Times bestselling author who lives in Minneapolis with her non-bank-robber husband. In her spare time she enjoys taking pictures of her cats, consuming boatloads of chocolate suckers, and tending her wild, bee-friendly garden.

newsletter:
http://annikamartinbooks.com/newletter

TikTok:
@annikamartinauthor

Facebook:
www.facebook.com/AnnikaMartinBooks

Instagram:
instagram.com/annikamartinauthor

website:
www.annikamartinbooks.com

Reader group of awesomeness
www.facebook.com/groups/AnnikaMartinFabulousGang/

Q: Did the bank robbers leave you satisfied? Desperately yearning? Saddled with a mysterious cartoon porn addiction?

A. Whatever the answer, I'm always so grateful when people leave reviews, even just a line or two. It helps readers find the books and it super helps the series.

PS: Thor sends kisses!

www.ingramcontent.com/pod-product-compliance
Lightning Source LLC
Chambersburg PA
CBHW061451210726
48287CB00007B/2457